DADDY'S BEST FRIEND

K.C. CROWNE

DESCRIPTION

17 years age gap.
Strictly off-limits.
Forbidden.
Taboo.

Why does something so wrong feel so right?
My dad's best friend is a single dad of twins...
And my secret crush.

I'm the only one who can clear his name...
But he's too scared to let me get close.

The uptight Mayor needs to relax...
And I'll do whatever it takes to loosen him up.

I'll prove there's no age restriction when it comes to lust...
Or to falling in love.

But there's one small problem...
I need to work up the courage reveal my secret...

That his twin daughters will soon have a baby brother or sister to share their daddy with!!

Warning: This taboo, older man romance is sure to leave your kindle on fire. Grab a cool beverage and enjoy this sweet forbidden romance.

ELLE

B*race yourself, Elle.*
    The sound of footsteps outside my office door grew louder and louder.

Butterflies fluttered in my belly.

"Eleanor. Mae. Shaeffer."

I recognized the raw and fiery passion in the man's deep manly voice.

Jeremiah Jenkins was the mayor of Liberty. Growing up, he insisted I call him Jeremiah, instead of Mr. Jenkins. He was also the man of my very wet dreams ever since I was old enough to dream about men. Too bad he was my late father's best friend, and far too loyal of a friend to cross the line with me.

Besides being handsome as sin, he was such an awesome guy. He never spoke to me like I was just a kid but talked to me like I was an adult.

I loved the sound of my full name escaping the scrumptious lips of my adolescent crush. If it were a song, I'd play that shit on repeat.

The door to my office swung open. As if seeing things in

slow-motion, I watched as the fine man sauntered in.

Hot ddddddamn!

Tall, built, and insanely handsome but now with a few light patches of grey on his head. It made him look even sexier than I remembered. How was that even possible?

His gaze had a kind of intensity. It was almost as if his striking blue eyes could touch me and I felt that touch *everywhere* on my body.

On my arms.

My legs.

My neck.

And especially on my nipples and in between my thighs.

I felt moisture gather at my center and soak the thin fabric of my panties. Even at the age of twenty-eight, my body was responding to him like a hormonal virgin. What was wrong with me? The man was old enough to be my father and I still felt this way about him, even years later.

Get it together, Elle.

Sure, I'd been turned on by other men in the past, but none of them had ever made me feel as hot and bothered as Jeremiah was doing at that very moment. Only a few minutes around him and he already had the strongest effect on me.

My cheeks warmed and flushed a bright red as I pressed my thighs together to find some relief.

Needing something to focus on other than the striking blue of his gaze, I cleared my throat and sorted the documents on my desk.

It was highly unlikely he felt the same way about me. While he was now a single dad, he always had plenty of grown and established women flocking for his affection.

"Yes?" I asked, cocking an eyebrow. "And it's nice to see you again too, Jeremiah. It's been awhile. Over five years? You're looking good. Keeping in shape, I see?"

He scowled at me, but he was still as handsome as he'd

ever been. It was hard not to squirm in my seat. Without breaking our eye contact, he took a deep breath and then opened those perfect lips.

"Young lady, do you know what you've done?"

Young lady.

My thighs rubbed together involuntarily, building pressure between my legs.

A shiver ran down my spine at the way he spoke, and I couldn't help but smile. The closer he got, the stronger the scent of his delicious cologne became.

I pulled a deep breath through my mouth and grew a bit taller in my spine. My new posture made my large boobs stick out a bit and, I could see Jeremiah forcing his gaze away from my ample cleavage.

I smiled.

Thank you Victoria Secret push-up bra.

His brow furrowed, the dark brows pushing together. Jeremiah might have a little more grey around the temples, but his hair was still as brown as I remembered it, and silky smooth. He wore it short as he always had because he couldn't be bothered to style it.

There was also a little silver sprinkled through his trimmed brown beard. His face looked younger than his forty-five years, even with the scowl.

That facial expression reminded me of the time he had to pick me up from a party, the one time in high school I'd decided to try alcohol. He was the reason I never touched the stuff again.

He threw a copy of the latest *Liberty Leader* on my desk. His face was plastered on the front, no less gorgeous in black and white than it was in color. The by-line on the article was, of course, my name. Eleanor Shaeffer.

My friends called me Elle. Jeremiah used to too, unless he was angry. And right now, he was *very* angry.

"Look I know this must have come as a surprise, but everything I wrote about you is positive and accurate. Why are you angry?"

"The fact that it's been well over five years since I've even seen you and our first interaction is after you've written an article on my personal life without my consent. How should I feel?"

"You make it sound like I painted you in a bad light."

"You know what I mean. This is all so out of character for you."

I leaned forward in amazement. "I left you several messages to approve the article but your staff never got back to me, even after I provided deadlines of its publication. The town wants to know their mayor, and I wrote what I knew. With the upcoming election, it's important to draw attention away from all the false drama in the news about you. I thought I had a realistic perspective that others might appreciate. It's my duty as a friend and a citizen of this town."

"You wrote about my daughters."

"I mentioned you have two little girls, but that's it. Beside the fact that you're a single dad. I mean, none of that is false, is it?"

His gaze narrowed on me, and he leaned closer.

"You're no longer a kid, Elle. We're in the real world and if I let myself get concerned about all the allegations about me then I probably shouldn't be a mayor anyway. Life isn't fair and we just need to focus on what we can control. You're better off not wasting your time, or mine."

He was back to calling me Elle, that was a good sign.

It made me sad to think about how jaded he must have become since the last time I'd seen him. Perhaps all the drama from the office had really gotten to him – and that coupled with his being a single dad to twins could make anyone feel fed-up.

On the good side, the scent of him was the same as when I was younger. Musky and natural, but delightful to my nostrils.

I closed my eyes for a second and inhaled the scent, taken back to a different time.

A time when my dad was alive.

Of BBQs on our back patio.

Flaunting my shapely bikini body around Jeremiah at the poolside.

I knew he had a distinct appreciation for curvaceous women. Compared to my classmates in school, I leaned on the side of curvy and voluptuous and I always loved that about my body.

When it came to Jeremiah, I didn't think twice about flaunting my curves. I yearned for his attention like a giddy little school girl.

Much to my disappointment, Jeremiah was always a gentleman. He never came even close to crossing the taboo line I yearned for him to cross. No matter how hard I tried, and boy did I try.

"Are you even listening to me?"

"Yes," I lied.

"Then what did I say?" He stared down at me with such a serious expression on his face that I burst out laughing.

"What's so funny?" He crossed his arms in front of his chest.

"Just that you remind me of my dad right now," I said, wiping the tear from my eye from laughing so hard. "So serious. So mad. You look like you're ready to burst a blood vessel or something."

He stared at me stone faced. He was always composed. Collected. I loved that about him. His composure was a galaxy away from the manners of all the immature boys I grew up around.

"I *am* mad."

"But why, Jeremiah?" My chair made a scratching sound as I scooted back from my desk. I stood up, but even standing, he still towered over me. He was at least a foot taller than me, but I didn't let that phase me. He had never scared me before, and I wasn't about to let him get to me now either. "You've always taught me to focus on the positive. It was all good, all very positive."

"When I'm ready to share my personal life in the media I want it by my terms, Elle." He placed his hands on the desk and leaned across.

I leaned forward too, my hands on the desk, mirroring him.

"Jeremiah, I hate to break it to you, but once you became a public figure, your personal life became fair game. And if I wasn't writing about you, then who would you prefer? Others are writing about you right now, and I'm sure you're aware it isn't all that good. I thought you could use some positive publicity for a change, considering all that's going on in the mayor's office right now, and talks of possible jail time. It's all too absurd for me to just stand around and not do anything!"

I didn't think it was possible for his frown to deepen, but he did it. Deep frown lines etched into his face, making him more attractive and adorable.

God, he's perfect.

"My daughters mean the world to me. And everything you know about me because of my friendship with your father is off limits, got it?"

Hot as sin and a great dad. How much more perfect can he be?

"Don't you want to get re-elected, Jeremiah? We need to distract the media from the shitstorm and showing that you're a good family man does exactly that."

Jeremiah's eyes fell. He stared down at my desk, at

nothing in particular. He didn't answer me. I gave him a good two minutes, and he didn't say a word.

Finally, he growled, "Please respect my wishes, Elle." He straightened himself and turned on his heels.

My eyes fell to his ass even though I knew I should behave myself.

Yep, still as tight as ever.

The years hadn't taken any sort of a negative toll on that man's body.

He didn't say anything more to me, just punctuated his point with a slamming of my office door. I stood at my desk for a moment, staring at the door. His scent lingered in the room, surrounding me like a familiar blanket.

I closed my eyes again, and this time, the memories came flooding through me.

"Come on, Elle. You're making words up now," Jeremiah barked. "Whizbang? Carl, get over here. Your daughter's cheating again."

I giggled. "Whizbang is a word! Look it up on that fancy smartphone of yours."

The year was 2007, and the first iPhone had just come out. Jeremiah had never been excited about the latest gadgets, but he was the owner of a big, fancy construction company. His contractors and insisted the phone would replace his laptop for work. He didn't even use the damn thing; it stayed in his pocket most of the time.

He nodded and pulled it out. "Alright, I'll do that."

"For the record, it's an adjective that means lively or sensational. It was also used during World War II. A small caliber, high velocity shell."

I watched as his eyes nearly popped from his skull. "How did you know that?"

I shrugged and took a sip from my lemonade and gave him a flirtatious blink. I was sixteen years old, still in high school, and I loved educating the older man. Especially since Jeremiah was smart - super smart. He had an engineering background, so math and science were more his forte.

Still, I loved impressing him with my vocabulary, and often learned new words just so I could have moments like this.

If only I had the words to articulate how I felt about him.

A knock on the door pulled me from the reverie.

"Yes?" I muttered, secretly hoping it was Jeremiah. I wanted nothing more than for him to come back into my office and tell me how happy he was to see me back in Liberty. To tell me he missed me and was so grateful for what I'd done.

But it wasn't Jeremiah. My assistant editor, Lucy, stood in the open doorway. "Is everything okay in here?"

"Yeah, everything's fine." I sat down at my desk, my gaze falling on the paper Jeremiah had left behind.

My pride and joy, my entire life's work, was wrapped up in that paper. As the owner and editor of the *Liberty Leader*, it was my responsibility to bring the news to the people. It has always been my dream - maybe not so much in Liberty, but I aged, I felt compelled to return to my roots.

This was where I was happiest in life and I wanted to return to that.

Especially after losing my dad.

Lucy took a seat across from me and saw the paper. Her face scrunched up as she read the headline and the first few lines. "What was he upset about? I don't get it."

A sigh escaped my lips. "It's a long story, Lucy. A very long story."

This newspaper was everything I had worked for. My dream. I should be happy; I had everything I needed. Yet something was still missing.

"Well, if it's any consolation, my mama always said that if

someone doesn't like what people say about them, maybe they should be a better person."

I frowned. "Jeremiah is already a good person. One of the best people I've met. That's the problem. I only wrote about the good things, the person I know and—"

Lucy wasn't getting it. The lights were on, sure, and she was watching me with her big, brown eyes, but not an ounce of what I was saying would matter to her. Unless you knew Jeremiah - *really* knew him - you wouldn't get it. He didn't open up to just anyone, and most people would never get to know the side of him I did.

"Never mind. Let's drop it. How's the article on the Liberty basketball team coming along?"

"It's coming along just fine. But, I mean they lost badly. We're writing about it anyway. There's not much else going on to replace it."

The question was did anyone really care? We weren't a sports town, which was fine. Our kids played basketball for fun, not glory. It kept the game a little purer, in my opinion.

"You know what? Nix it. Don't write about them losing. Maybe interview the coach instead, talk to him about the teamwork or something else. Don't focus on the negative."

"But it's the news," Lucy said.

"Yes, but let's be honest, Lucy, It'll only bring the kids down, and this town doesn't need another disappointment."

I sighed and rubbed my temples. The fact was, print journalism was on the way out, and no one really cared about it much anyway. Liberty was small enough that everyone knew what was going on without picking up a paper. It was tradition for many families to do so, the older citizens, of course. But the younger generation had yet to pick up on that habit, if they ever would.

I was on a sinking ship, and I knew it. I knew it when I bought the paper from Jasper Townsend, but I thought I could turn it around. I thought there'd be some kind of news, talking to the local businesses, exploring the beauty of Liberty, and of course, covering the good side of politics.

Like how people like Jeremiah had real aspirations for our town.

"Sales down again?" Lucy asked, reminding me that she was still in the room.

"Sales were never up to begin with."

"I'm sure something will work out."

She was so sweet and naive, much like I was when I entered the industry. I became a journalist to try and make a difference in the world, to share the news and to hopefully open people's eyes to the world around them.

The one thing that kept me getting out of bed was doing everything I could to keep our town from losing one of the best mayors we've had in decades, especially if there was something I could do to get him out of his own damn way.

Jeremiah didn't want me involved, but this was about much more than our relationship.

Both he and my dad taught me to hold tight to what I believed in, no matter the odds. I wasn't going to give up, not without a fight.

Jeremiah Jenkins may have been jaded by life from one too many disappointments, but I still believed that good could prosper evil.

He dedicated most of his life to others. It was my turn to be there for him.

And if I was being 100% truthful, it was my opportunity to once and for all prove that was much more than just a kid.

I was going to go after what I wanted, and I wasn't going to give up.

JEREMIAH

I arrived home well before I needed to pick up my girls from day-care.

Removing my clothes, I crossed my bedroom and made a beeline for my shower. Not even bothering with the hot water, I cranked the cold all the way and stepped underneath the massive rainwater spray.

The cold water fell onto my skin like needles, but I didn't dare to warm it up. I needed the cold and the sobering effect it provided.

"What the fuck was that?" I muttered to myself as I thought back on my conversation with Elle.

I got what I wanted from our meeting and made my point about the news story clear. There was only one problem with me seeing her after five years - and I could feel it pulsing between my damn legs.

Never, not even in my wildest dreams had I imagined that the shy, awkward, scrabble-loving teenager I had once known would turn into a vixen with perfectly round hips, full tits, and the face of an angel.

To top everything off, she was smart, funny, and strong-willed in a way most women I came across weren't.

She was one of those whole package women, except that she wasn't. She couldn't be.

At least, not for me.

She was Carl's, daughter, and no matter how hot she was or how much my cock twitched at the thought of her, that was all she could ever be.

I groaned and straightened my body so that every inch of me would be under the frigid spray. Defying the laws of nature, my cock didn't shrink at the cold. It remained awake and ready for someone that could never be mine.

My eyes closed in an attempt to focus my brain and find a solution to the problem. However, all I thought about was Elle.

Instinctively, my hand drifted down to my massive erection. Behind my closed lids, I saw Elle's sweet mouth wrapped around my cock. I wondered how much of me she would be able to take and how deliciously smooth it would feel. I pictured her tits bouncing and her pretty hair wrapped around my hand as I worked myself in and out of her lips.

I knew that even fantasizing about her was wrong, but for some reason, the forbidden aspect of it made the whole thing even sweeter.

Before I knew it, my balls were tight, and my body felt like it was dangling from a precipice. I held onto the wall in front of me and kept Elle's face and tits front and center in my mind as I sped up my movements, until my body finally erupted with one of the strongest orgasms I'd ever had.

Once I was done, and she was still in my thoughts, I stood under the cold water waiting for my breath to return to normal and realized one very true fact: I was *incredibly fucked.*

~

I pulled my coat around me as a crisp breeze filtered down the street, blowing up snow in its wake. The blanket of whiteness over the earth was as much a staple of the town as the local businesses.

We were, after all, in the mountains.

Liberty's Main Street awaited me when I stepped out of my car. Everything was within walking distance downtown, if it could even be called a downtown at all. A few local shops, a B&B, a day-care, a café, and, the local paper. There were a few other little shops and diners. Most of them had been there as long as I could remember.

I inhaled the cold, Utah air. It was cold enough to almost hurt the lungs. If you weren't born and bred for that kind of weather, it might be a bit too much. Some folks didn't care much for snow and cold, but I preferred it over the heat out west and the humidity in the east.

Utah was my home; Liberty was Heaven on Earth, as far as I was concerned.

It came with its share of small town drama, but I was grateful to be raising my daughters in the town I grew up in.

I trekked the block to Little Cubs.

I thought about my meeting with Elle the day before and had to adjust my pants from the erection that was coming.

Shit just the thought of her has me screwed up.

She'd grown into such a beautiful woman.

And the curves on her.

Shit.

She'd always been a curvy girl but I never thought about her as more than my best friend's daughter. *Until now.*

Now, everything about her blew me away.

She was just a little too focused on her career and didn't see the bigger picture around her.

Or maybe I just had a thing against journalists. She might be a good one, but as far as I was concerned, she was amongst parasites and leeches. It was far too easy for them to suck you into their world.

Plus, it had been a long ass time since I last saw her.

It was hard to believe that beautiful, blonde-haired, brown-eyed woman with the perfect figure was Carl's little Ellie-bean. As soon as she'd turned eighteen, she'd run off to New York City and blossomed from a child to a woman.

I was sure the men in New York had been all over her - she was a stunner. She could have been a model, but anytime anyone had mentioned it to her, she scrunched up her perfectly upturned nose and said she wanted to use her brain, not her beauty, to get ahead in the world.

It was hard to believe the woman in that office was the same girl I used to play Scrabble with, who'd always manage to come up with the most obscure words to beat me. Sometimes I let her win...no, that was a lie. She always won fair and square; I just didn't like to admit that a little girl could beat me at a game.

But she was smarter than anyone else I'd met, and I met a lot of people. I only wished she'd used her smarts for something other than writing about my personal life.

"Good afternoon, Mayor," a voice pulled me from my thoughts.

I looked around and found an older woman, a face I recognized. "Well hello there, Mrs. Wilson." I continued walking, my focus on the door of the day-care.

"I read about you in the paper. That was a real good story. I mean the recent article that seemed to paint you in a more realistic light. I enjoyed it a lot. You're a good man for taking in those babies, you know."

"They're my daughters. I didn't adopt them off the street or anything." Mrs. Wilson flinched as if I'd slapped her, and I realized my tone was a bit rough. "Sorry, what I mean is - I'm no hero. Just a father, that's all."

"Well, you're a lot like *your* father, so I say that makes you a hero. But what do I know?" She shrugged her shoulders and continued walking away before I could argue with her.

I was no damn hero.

Just a man trying to live his life, raise his daughters, and leave my personal life out of the damn limelight. But thanks to Elle's article, everyone would think they knew me and my little girls.

I pulled open the door to Little Cubs and heard laughter. I'd always loved the sound of children laughing, but never thought I'd be hearing it in my own home. Sure, the girls were too young for laughing, but one day, the halls would be filled with it.

Tabitha, one of the teachers, was on the floor with toddlers all around her. She glanced up and smiled. "One second, Jeremiah. Piper should be right with you."

Piper was the owner of the day-care and also happened to be one of Elle's best friends growing up.

Shit, another reason I won't be able to get Elle out of my damn head.

With Liberty being such a small town it was hard not to be acquainted with people in the same circles.

Like Elle, I remembered when Piper was no taller than some of the little ones surrounding Tabitha. It was weird to think of her all grown up and responsible enough to be watching other people's kids, but she did a damn fine job of it.

Piper scurried from the back, a smile on her face.

"Hey! That was the quickest work emergency I've ever seen."

"Yes, just a quick meeting, then I had some errands to run." I frowned when I thought about what 'business' I really had to take care of after my run in with Elle in her office.

I cleared my throat.

"How are the girls?"

It had been their first week in day-care, and I was a little stressed about that. I was trying to find a nanny, but so far, none of the people I'd interviewed fit the bill. I'd known Piper forever, and I trusted her, but it was still hard leaving my children for the first time. At least she wasn't a stranger.

"Oh, they're angels," she cooed, her hand over her heart. "And they were just fine, don't you worry. Want to come back with me? I can help you carry them out?"

I nodded and followed Piper down the hallway to where the infants were kept. It had already been two months since I'd brought them home, and I still couldn't believe it. I never expected to be a dad at all, much less to twin girls.

"I do hope you'll reconsider and think about working with us in the future."

"I appreciate you, Piper. I do. I think you're highly qualified and run a top-notch day-care, but with everything going on, I'd feel more comfortable with someone watching them from home. I hope you understand."

She nodded, her smile unphased. "I get it, I do. We're always here for you. You know that."

"Thank you." I didn't mention how I needed help at home too. One child was hard enough, but two? During feedings and diaper changes, when they were both screaming, it was hard. I was outnumbered and had gained a new respect for single parents.

Piper pulled open the door to the nursery and we stepped inside. Frannie was in the corner changing a baby. She turned her head and smiled when she saw me, immediately gushing, "Oh, your little girls are the sweetest!"

"Thank you." I was always being told this, but I had no

idea how to respond. I wasn't sure how bad two-month-olds could actually be for any frame of reference. So I just nodded and smiled and said thanks. I hated leaving the girls, but as mayor, it was sometimes unavoidable.

The mere sight of my twin girls melted my cold heart. It was like their presence just melted all the stresses of my day away. They always had that effect on me.

Elle asked me if I wanted to get re-elected. Truth be told, I didn't. I hated the job. I'd taken it out of obligation. It was meant to be a short-term solution after my father died, until someone suitable stepped up. No one suitable stepped up. So I remained mayor of the city I loved. I only did it because I loved Liberty; I had no desire to be in the public light. I had never wanted a career in politics. I had no idea how to run a city.

Now, with my daughters at home, I especially hated leaving them. They'd been through enough and needed a stable household. It was my responsibility to give them that. And I didn't take that responsibility lightly.

I just wanted to keep my beloved hometown out of the wrong hands, and so far, I'd been successful, but my time was coming to an end.

And as much as I should worry about my competitor, part of me just wanted to step down and be done with it. I wanted to focus on my girls and maybe get back to running my construction business. Or retire. With my finances in order, that was also an option for me, but I wasn't sure I'd ever be ready to stop working. Not at forty-five. Though I'd already made more money than I would ever need, I still had a lot of life left in me.

Piper carried Grace, while I carried Amelia. She made small talk, which I hardly paid attention to, as we walked to my truck.

Piper helped snap Grace into her car seat while I took

care of Amelia. I was grateful for the help wherever I could get it. It often felt like I needed to grow another set of hands, which was one reason I wanted to find a nanny, someone to help me since their mother wasn't in the picture. But I was too picky. Whoever I chose would have to be as careful as I was, to love them like I did, and I just didn't think it was possible to find that in what was essentially an employee.

Perhaps I was being too picky, but they were my girls. My responsibility.

"Thanks, Piper," I said, patting the young woman on the back. "I appreciate all your help."

"No problem. I'm always around if you need me to keep an eye on them," she offered. She started to say something, but stopped and smiled instead.

I'm sure she wanted to know what the work emergency was about. Everyone did. I was the talk of the town ever since one of my staff members spread rumours that I had taken bribes from the developers looking to mine the valuable lithium from the ground. Then he'd left town. Or so we thought.

James Fitzhenry had been our city treasurer. He hadn't been seen in a month, shortly after he spoke about the supposed bribes. Poof. One day he was there, the next he was gone.

Now I knew why.

When it became obvious I wasn't going to talk about what kept me busy for the day, Piper excused herself with a friendly smile. "Drive safely, Jeremiah."

She hurried back into the warmth of *Little Cubs*, and I climbed into my truck to get it started and warmed for my girls. They were covered in blankets, but since they couldn't wear their thick coats in their car seats, I blasted the heat up and hoped the truck warmed quickly.

You girls deserve the world. God as my witness I will do every-thing I can to give you that and more.

～

"Shh," I whispered, rocking Grace in my arms while holding a bottle for Amelia at the same time. I wished I was an octopus, especially at feeding time. These two wiggly little bodies were hard to handle at the same time, and it never failed that when I was feeding one, the other would get fussy - either impatient for food or if they'd already been fed, from gas or boredom or God knows what.

Sometimes I wondered if I'd made a mistake. Staring at their sweet faces, with my mother's nose and my father's eyes, I knew I wanted them. But was I being selfish? Could someone else raise them better than me? Would an adoptive family have offered them a better life than I could?

Hell no.

My heart ached just thinking about it.

They'd only been in my life for two months, but it was already hard to imagine life without them. They were my world, and I would do anything for them - even give up my role as Liberty's mayor so I could be the best father possible. They deserved it.

I dropped the bottle as I adjusted Grace in my arms, her screaming sounding so heart wrenching. I wished I knew the magic formula to make it stop, to make her happy. I felt so lost. Amelia started whimpering, and I grabbed the bottle and held it to her mouth as well. I needed to put Grace down to properly feed Amelia, but it pained me to do so.

A knock at my door surprised me; I wasn't expecting anyone. I groaned and contemplated not answering, but at the meeting at work that day, I was told the police may be stopping by to question me at any time. They could probably hear the babies crying and knew I was home. It wouldn't look good to avoid them when they suspected me of several crimes.

"One second," I called out, hoping they could hear me over the noise.

I placed Grace in her pack and play and hurried to the door. When it swung it open, I was surprised to not find the police, but Elle. She was still in her work attire - a tailored grey dress suit that fit her curvy body perfectly. A soft pink, silk shirt showed under her jacket, with a pink, grey, and white scarf tied around her neck loosely, pulling the look together.

She'd always knew how to dress, but this was not the Elle I remembered from years before. While she was tall and fit, she also had curves in all the right places, making sure there was no doubt in anyone's mind that she was a grown woman.

Her blonde hair was pulled back in a bun, completing the sexy businesswoman look.

I found myself wanting to release it from its confines and watch it tumble around her shoulders.

Grab her hair in my fist and pull her lips to mine.

"Listen," she said, not meeting my gaze. "I feel really bad about our talk earlier. Can I come in so we can talk?"

"It's not a good time."

She looked past me into the house. "Do you need some help?"

Before I could lie and tell her no, she pushed past me and into the living room. She made a beeline toward the crying, like a moth drawn to a flame and I couldn't help but watch the sway of her perfect ass as she went. The girls were in pack and play sleepers in the living room. She walked over to Grace, who was crying the loudest, and picked her up.

"Oh my gosh, Jeremiah. They're beautiful."

I was at her side; ready to show her how to hold the baby

if needed, but she didn't need my help. She rocked Grace in her arms, speaking to her in hushed tones, and the baby's cries quieted rather quickly. My cock twitched again at the how good she was with my daughter.

"How did you do that?"

"Huh?" Elle seemed to have been lost in a fantasy, shook her head, and met my gaze.

"I've been trying forever to get her to calm down," I said. "And you just walk in here and stop her crying in seconds."

"Babies can sense our stress, Jeremiah," she said matter-of-factly.

"I'm not stressed."

Yeah, right. Who the hell am I kidding?

She gave me a look that said she knew I was lying. Amelia let out a soft whimper which turned to more crying, drawing our attention.

"I was in the middle of feeding them," I muttered, going to Amelia and picking her up to give her a bottle.

"Alright, can I help?" Elle asked me.

I'd originally made both of their bottles, not thinking. I motioned to Grace's bottle sitting on the coffee table. "Do you know how to feed a baby?"

"Do I know how to feed a baby?" she asked in a mocking tone. "Come on, Jeremiah. I used to babysit all the freaking time in high school and continued doing it in college too. I even nannied for a wealthy family for a while to pay for school. You know that."

She picked up the bottle and began feeding Grace as if it was second nature.

"Alright, I'm sorry. They're just my babies. I'm a little overprotective."

"Of course you are. I'm not surprised at all."

"What do you mean?"

"Well, you were always protective of me, and I wasn't

even your daughter." She shrugged and took a seat on my sofa, her attention focused on the bundle in her arms.

In case I could forget that she was my best friend's daughter, well, there she was to remind me.

Grace's tiny fingers gripped the scarf, and if Elle minded, she didn't let it show. Knowing Elle, her clothing wasn't cheap.

"So which one do I have?" she asked me, though she didn't look up.

"You have Grace," I murmured softly, taking a seat in the chair across from her. "She has a birthmark on her right hand, right by her thumb. She's also smaller."

"Grace, after your mother," she whispered.

"Yes."

"And Amelia after your grandmother," she said, looking at the baby in my arms.

"Yes, right again."

"You always were a sentimental man," she said with a playful smile. "Even if you try to hide it."

I couldn't really argue that. My mother and my grandmother had played a big role in my life. Both women were gone, but I knew they'd have been so happy to see me as a father. Surprised, too. My mother had passed only a couple years prior, and I was her only child. She had always assumed our family would stop with me. But she'd been wrong. Not that anyone could have expected that I'd one day be the father of twin girls, especially at my age.

"So do you forgive me?" Elle asked, her brown eyes wide and innocent. "About the article, I mean."

I thought for a moment. Truthfully, I couldn't stay mad at her for long. She was Carl's daughter, and nothing she ever did could make me hate her. Even if she was a journalist.

"Yes, but please come to me before writing anything else in the future. And my daughters are off limits. Got it?"

"Got it," she said. "I'll respect your wishes, Jeremiah. I just wanted to help."

"I know."

She was like her father. Carl was quick to anger because he was passionate - like Elle. He also had a good heart, but he always thought he knew what was right for someone else. Elle took after him more than I could have imagined.

"George Holt is a terrible man," Elle commented, frowning. "Like, really bad. There's no way he can be mayor of Liberty."

"I know."

Elle seemed relieved that I agreed with her. I knew George well enough to know that he had an agenda. He had been a developer himself, and he'd been trying for years to grow Liberty into a tourist town to rival some of the other ski towns in the U.S. But the townspeople didn't want that. It would mean the raising of rents, many would likely be displaced, and small businesses would be replaced with large corporations. We favoured our local coffee shops over Starbucks. It's what made Liberty what it was.

George wasn't born and raised there; he didn't get it. He was everything Liberty wasn't, and there was no way he would win the election. Unless no one ran against him. As the current mayor, taking over after my father died in office, it was a given that I'd run for re-election and win. Until the latest scandal.

We finished feeding the babies, but Elle continued holding and rocking Grace gently as we talked mostly about frivolous things. Elle always could carry a conversation all on her own.

"I think Grace might be getting sleepy," she said, her voice low.

"Amelia too," I commented, noting the little girl's eyelids drifting closed. "It's about their bedtime anyway."

I stood, and Elle did too. She followed me to their nursery at the end of the hallway, next to my bedroom. She stared around the room, her mouth opening as she saw the cribs. The baby beds were ornate and heavy, well-made and sturdy. Above each twin's crib was their name, carved in wood. Amelia's was painted in purple, my grandma's favorite color, and Grace was painted a soft blue, my mother's favorite.

"Wow, did you make these?" Elle asked, running her hand over the crib.

"I did." I smiled as I watched her trace the name above Grace's crib. "I made everything in here, actually."

"I knew you were good with woodworking, but wow," she breathed. She placed Grace down in the bed and stared at her for a bit, a small smile on her face.

I did the same with Amelia, watching as she fell into a deep sleep. I turned on the baby monitors and motioned for Elle to follow me out. I pulled the door, but left it open just a smidge so a small light from the hallway could creep in.

We walked back into the living room, and I thought that might be it. Elle had apologized. I forgave her. We put the kids to bed. Now she could leave.

But she sat down on the couch again, heaving a sigh. "You don't happen to have anything to drink, do you?"

"I might have some beer in the fridge." I scratched my beard.

"Ooh, can I have one?"

My first instinct was to tell her no, that she was too young. But she wasn't too young anymore. She was a grown woman, not Carl's little girl.

"Sure," I said, making my way into the kitchen. I grabbed one for her, then decided it wouldn't hurt to have one now that the girls were down. Only one.

I opened the bottles and walked back into the living

room, handing one to Elle before taking my place in the large leather chair across from her again.

She drank from the bottle before giggling. "It feels weird to be drinking around you, ever since that time you picked me up from the party. You know, I don't drink much these days, thanks to you."

"Good, I'm glad my talk stuck with you."

"It did," she said, turning the bottle around in her hands. "I mean, that and my daddy yelling at me, but you talked to me like an adult. I really appreciated that." She took another swig, made a face and put the bottle on the table.

"You were sixteen. Not yet an adult, but not a child either."

"My father didn't think like so. He still thought I was a child." She spoke softly, her eyes glazing over. I knew she had to miss her father. We all did, but she had a special bond with him. She was daddy's little girl.

But it was hard to imagine her as anyone's little girl now.

She pulled off the scarf, tossing it on the table before taking off her jacket. "Sorry, it's a bit warm. Do you mind?"

"No, of course not."

She placed her jacket on the couch next to her. Her silky pink shirt clung to her body. It didn't go all the way down to her skirt either, showing off just a hint of her stomach.

I took a quick swig of my beer, trying to distract myself. I couldn't look at her body, what was I doing? She was my best friend's daughter.

Elle crossed her legs, and her skirt rode up, showing off her toned thighs. She had always been into yoga and keeping herself in shape, even though she didn't work out too much. She was no athlete, just liked to keep herself healthy.

I put the beer down, afraid it was clouding my thoughts. I had to adjust in my seat, cringing as my erection brushed against my jeans. I cursed myself; that's what I got for having such horribly inappropriate thoughts about Elle.

Thankfully, she didn't seem to notice and continued talking. "Do you remember that time Dad thought I took a drink from his beer? When I was eight, maybe?"

"I do," I chuckled, remembering Carl's face. He wasn't so much mad as he was worried. "He kept asking me to call poison control to make sure it wouldn't hurt you. You kept insisting you'd only smelled it and thought it was gross."

"That's exactly what happened. I smelled it, thought it smelled like pee, and put it right back down."

"And Carl kept saying, 'It's okay if you tried it, you won't be in trouble. I just need to know in case it can make you sick'"

"Yes! He really was a good dad." Her voice cracked.

"He was. I hope to be as good as him."

"Oh, I have no doubt. I always thought you'd make an amazing father."

I looked down at my hand. "Thank you. That means a lot coming from you."

A silence hung over us. I glanced up and found her staring at me, a pained look on her face.

"What's wrong?"

"Do you think—never mind." She shook her head as if trying to banish whatever thoughts she was having.

"Do I think what?"

She hesitated, but I could tell the words were on the tip of her tongue. Finally, she sighed. "Do you think my father was proud of me?"

Tears welled in her eyes, and it killed me. Any sexual thoughts I'd had went right out the window. This was Carl's little girl. This was Eleanor.

"Of course, Elle," I murmured. "How could he not be?"

"I don't know. He just had all these big dreams for me, for

me to go off to college in New York City, to become this big-time journalist. It was supposed to be worth being gone for so long. I even missed—" She stopped short, but I knew what she was thinking.

"Elle, there's no way you could have known he was going to pass away so quickly. No one did. He showed no signs, no symptoms, and even if he suspected it, you know your father was far too stubborn to let anyone know something was wrong."

She nodded. "I guess so. I feel like I missed so much, and I still ended up here. But it's too late. He's not here."

I wanted to cross the room and hug her but wasn't sure it was appropriate. I also didn't trust my thoughts since only moments before I'd gotten an erection looking at her. Jesus, I couldn't be sure what would happen if I actually touched her.

So I stayed put, tried to comfort her from afar. "Elle, your father just wanted you to be happy. He didn't care what you did with your life, as long as you were happy and healthy - and you are, aren't you?"

She nodded. "For the most part, yes. Except for his absence, I really do love being home."

"And he would be proud of you for taking over the *Leader*."

She barked out a laugh. "Proud of me running that pitiful excuse for a paper, you mean? Not like we're going to be in business much longer. No one wants to read the local paper anymore."

"He'd be proud of you because you took a chance. You took ownership of your life and didn't let your doubts stop you."

She was silent for a second, and a smile crossed her face. "Thanks, Jeremiah. You knew my father better than anyone, so it means a lot to hear that. You always could get through to me."

She stood up, and before I could stop her, she crossed the room, leaned down toward me, and wrapped her arms over my shoulders. Her breasts pressed nearly into my face since she was standing and I was sitting. It was hard to breathe, hard to think for a second. She pulled away, and the erection was back.

Thankfully, she didn't look down. She looked straight in my eyes instead.

"I think I'm going to head out, but thank you for the talk. I've missed you, you know that?"

"I've missed you too," I admitted.

Calm down, Jeremiah. This is Carl's daughter, I kept repeating to myself.

I walked her to the door, and she gave me a proper hug. I swallowed hard, worried that she'd feel my erection against her body. But when she pulled away, she seemed oblivious. She leaned in and kissed me on the cheek, her soft lips brushing against my skin and sending the rest of the blood in my body south.

Get a grip, Jeremiah. Get a fucking grip. This is unacceptable.

Elle pulled away, and there was something in her eyes - a heat that I'd never seen before from her.

"Have a good night," I said, yanking the door open. "And drive safely. Your father would never forgive me if anything happened to you."

I brought up her father, hoping to remind both of us both of who she was to me. Her gaze fell and her cheeks flushed.

"Yes, of course. Have a good night, Jeremiah."

She walked out the door, and I realized she'd left her scarf on my couch. But I wasn't going to risk calling her back.

ELLE

"P sst," Lucy hissed, poking her head in my office the next day. "I heard from a little bird that there was a big secret meeting at the mayor's office yesterday."

"Do tell," I said, motioning for Lucy to come in.

She stepped inside, shutting the door behind her. She took a seat across from me, leaning in as if telling me a secret in a room full of people. "Well, as you know, Peter Montgomery and I are pretty close these days."

Peter was essentially her boyfriend and held an administrative role in the mayor's office.

"He told me they suspect James didn't just run off to protect himself, but that he's dead. They found a body; they're waiting for the police to identify it."

I cocked an eyebrow. "James Fitzhenry?"

"Who else?" she asked.

"The whistle-blower? He might be dead?" My heart sunk at those words. I didn't know James too well, but I didn't care for him much. Not only because he was the one who spoke out against Jeremiah, but also because he'd dated George Holt's daughter. Still, I didn't wish death upon anyone.

I also feared what it might mean for Jeremiah.

"Mmhmm, and they say the FBI might be getting involved."

I leaned back in my chair, feeling numb. "Wow."

"I know, right?" Lucy seemed to be on the edge of her seat, as if this were some murder mystery television show.

"Lucy, this is real life. This is our town, and someone from our town could be dead, while another man may be investigated for crimes he didn't commit."

Lucy cocked her head to the side. "How come you're so certain Jeremiah is innocent?"

"Because I know him. I know what type of man he is."

"Are you sure you know the real him, though? Maybe you know—"

"I know him, Lucy," I snapped.

"Fine, alright." She held her hands up to surrender. "I'm just saying—"

"You're jumping to conclusions along with everyone else. That's not responsible reporting. We don't run a tabloid here. We wait for facts."

Lucy's gaze narrowed. "I don't mean to be so bold, but are you sure your personal relationship with Jeremiah might not be clouding your judgement here? Maybe a bit?"

"Innocent until proven guilty," I reminded her. "We stand by that philosophy here. If you have a problem with that, maybe the *National Enquirer* is hiring."

Lucy snapped her lips shut and frowned. "I didn't mean we'd report on anything that wasn't factually true."

"Good. Then we're done here."

Lucy stood up carefully, and I could tell she wanted to continue the conversation. She was proud of herself for having the gossip. I hated gossip that wasn't backed up by fact. She should have known better than to run her mouth to me without proof.

Except I had a feeling she was right. Peter did work in city government. As soon as Lucy was gone, I grabbed the phone and dialed Jeremiah's office number.

A friendly female voice picked up. "Office of Mayor Jenkins. This is Mary speaking. How may I help you?"

"Hi Mary. This is Elle Schaeffer. Is Jeremiah in?"

"No, he's not, I'm afraid. I can give him a message, but he's not open to talking to the press right now."

"This isn't a press issue," I insisted. I wanted to argue with Mary, tell her that Jeremiah was like family to me, but I dropped it. I knew a better way to reach him. I thanked her and said goodbye, then hung up and dialed his cell phone.

Jeremiah's gruff voice answered on the second ring. "Elle?"

I told him everything Lucy had told me, which wasn't much. Jeremiah remained quiet when I finished, and I thought maybe we'd lost our connection. "Jeremiah?"

"I'm here."

"Can you verify any of that?"

"Not to the press, no."

"It's off the record, I promise."

He sighed. "I don't want to talk about it, Elle. It's nothing personal, but I'd rather not talk about it with anyone - even if it's on a personal level."

"Jeremiah, are you in trouble?"

"Of course not. It's all a misunderstanding. I didn't take bribes, and I sure as hell didn't kill anyone. The truth will come to light soon enough."

"Is James dead?" He didn't answer me. "Jeremiah!"

"Elle, I said I don't want to talk about it. I'm not even sure I *can* talk about it yet, press or not. So please, respect that."

The line went dead and I slammed my phone down on my desk.

"Dammit." I wasn't cursing because Jeremiah wouldn't

work with me; I was worried about him. What had started as nothing but some rumors turned into so much more, and I didn't like Jeremiah's neck on the chopping block.

I only wanted to help. Couldn't he see that?

I leaned back in my chair, rubbing my temples. It wasn't even lunch time and already I was on the verge of a migraine. And just when I thought the day couldn't get any worse, there was a knock on my door.

"Yes?"

My administrative assistant, Taylor, spoke up from the other side of the door. "There's someone here to see you."

"Tell them to call me and make an appointment—"

I was cut off by someone opening the door. The woman who stepped into my office wasn't my admin, but I recognized her. And my day just went from bad to worse.

I stumbled to my feet, taken off guard. "Ms. Holt, I wasn't expecting you today."

Lauren Holt was all legs. Without heels, she was probably 5'8" or so, but she always wore heels, the tallest ones she could find. Her blonde hair was impeccably colored - highlights and lowlights in all the right places, and not a stray strand of hair on her head.

Lauren's painted lips were pursed, her hands on her hips, her perfectly manicured nails tapping on her hip. I reached out a hand to shake hers, as a professional courtesy, but she didn't take it. I dropped my hand and steeled myself.

"To what do I owe the pleasure?" I spoke through gritted teeth. She knew as well as I did that I wasn't pleased to see her. We never had liked each other.

She took a seat across from me, crossing her legs as if she was trying to show off her perfect calves. She was in a designer suit, perfectly tailored to her body. She looked at me pointedly. "I read your article on Jeremiah Jenkins."

"Okay." I sat down at my desk. "And you're here why?"

"Because you need to give my father the same attention you've given Jeremiah," she stated matter-of-factly.

"I have written about your father."

"Nothing to the same caliber as the article on Jeremiah," she retorted, uncrossing her legs and crossing them again as if she couldn't get comfortable. I rather enjoyed her discomfort; I certainly wasn't comfortable with her there.

"Well, I grew up with Jeremiah. I know him. I have more material to work with." It was also easier to paint him in a positive light, considering he wasn't an asshole, but I kept that part to myself. I could be professional when I had to be.

Lauren sighed and waved her hand as if to dismiss me. "Please, you don't even try to talk to my father. It's clear you're biased, which is incredibly unprofessional as a journalist, as you know. You're letting your personal relationship with Jeremiah cloud your judgement, and you're not living up to your duties as impartial press. You owe the people a fair and balanced view."

As much as I hated to admit it, she was right. I tried not to let my personal relationships get in the way of the job, but even if Jeremiah had been a complete stranger, I think I'd have preferred him. The competitor was truly awful, which was the real reason I hadn't tried to talk to him more. Every time I did, I left with my blood boiling and a desire to punch something. It made it nearly impossible to write an unbiased piece on the man.

But I owed the people fair and balanced reporting.

"Alright, what do you propose?" I tried to keep the annoyance out of my voice. I may have even succeeded.

"An interview with my father at his home with his family so you can see what type of man he is outside of the office."

"Fine."

Lauren raised her perfectly arched eyebrows in surprise. "Really? You're going along with it that easily?"

I held up my hands in defeat. "You're right. I should present both sides equally. I'll meet with your father in his home and see him as you and your brother do."

A look crossed her face that I couldn't read, not clearly. She scrunched up her nose in disgust, but only for a moment. Sometimes it felt like she hated her father as much as the rest of us, but if you didn't know how to read people, you'd have missed the tics.

Maybe I'd get to see how Lauren really felt about her father. Or maybe I'd see another act. I felt like that's all they were - an act. They pretended to be a perfect family unit for the press, but something didn't sit right for me. I was actually looking forward to this opportunity, not just for journalistic integrity, but to see if my gut was right about Lauren really despising her dad, even though she put on a front to the press.

She was, after all, delegated to PR while her brother was being groomed for a career in politics, working as Daddy's campaign manager. I always wondered how Lauren felt about that, but we weren't close enough for me to ask.

But maybe I'd get to see for myself.

Ooo000ooo

George and Elizabeth Holt had at least two homes in the Liberty area. One was a smaller house, near downtown, that I swear was just for show. It always looked empty to me, and I believe they only owned it to appear to be living within city limits.

I met them at their other home, the one just outside of

Liberty, where there was more land to build their massive estate.

I'd never been to the Holt home before, never had a need. They'd lived in Liberty on-and-off for most of my life, but I didn't recall them ever really being around that much. And I couldn't fathom why when I pulled into their circle driveway.

Their home was the size of some small towns. It almost looked like they'd picked up a Southern plantation home and dropped it in the middle of Utah. The home towered over the landscape, nearly blocking the gorgeous mountains from view from the front. There was a wrap-around porch around the house, which was three stories, at least. Likely with some underground garages for Daddy's car collection. He was a known collector of classic cars, much like some people collect knickknacks. He was often seen driving through town in a new car; he had a different one for each day of the month, it seemed. All of them expensive - Porsche, Jaguar, Rolls Royce, Bentley.

I always wondered why someone with his kind of money would return to Liberty. His family had lived elsewhere for years, until about two or three years ago when they started work on their mansion outside of town. Maybe they had decided to retire here, come back home. I didn't know. I didn't really care either. I just wished they'd stayed gone. People like them weren't good for Liberty, I feared.

Especially since George Holt had an agenda for our small town. One that didn't fit with our beliefs here.

As soon as I parked my car, an attendant rushed over. "Welcome, Ms. Schaeffer," the attendant said. "I'm happy to park your car for you."

"It can stay here," I told him. "I'm not blocking anything."

"As you wish," the man said, nodding and motioning for me toward the house. "May I escort you inside?"

"Sure," I said with a polite smile.

The man was dressed as a stereotypical butler. I had no idea they really dressed like that in real life. The fact that they even had help was shocking to me because it was not a common thing in Liberty, outside a nanny or maybe a house cleaner that came out once or twice a month. But the Holts had an entire staff that would rival that of royalty.

In their mind, they thought they were royalty.

I followed the butler up the stairs and toward the gigantic wooden door. It had to have taken several elephants to move that door into place. The door was almost two stories in and of itself, with a handle the size of my head. All wood, thick and strong. As if George Holt and family had to protect themselves from the outside world, much like a fortress.

The butler pulled open the door, thankfully, since it looked heavy as hell. He motioned for me to enter. "After you, Miss."

"Thank you."

As soon as I stepped inside, I felt like I had left Liberty and entered a castle somewhere foreign. The foyer led to a spiral staircase that seemed to go up forever, with a landing in the middle to stop and rest upon before proceeding up the top. That landing was bigger than my bedroom. A red and gold runner ran up the staircase. A crystal chandelier hung over us, made up of about a thousand large crystals, all sparkling from the light. It was nearly blinding.

There was also an elevator to the left of the grand staircase. It looked like something from a 1920s hotel. Very classy. I'd never been inside a house with an elevator before.

"Right this way," the butler said, leading me onward.

We didn't go up the big stairs or use the elevator, to my dismay. Instead, we took a right and went into an enormous formal living room. It was hard to imagine anyone actually lived here, as it looked impeccable, like something from a magazine. There wasn't a stray cup or even a book out of place. No television. Just a stone fireplace that nearly took up one entire wall with a family portrait - painted, of course - hanging over the mantle. A series of couches and chairs, all burgundy with gold accents, were strategically placed around the fireplace and an oriental rug was in the center of the room.

"The Holts will be joining you shortly," the butler said.

He sauntered off, leaving me alone in the grand room that felt as staged and fake as the people I was about to interview.

Keep an open mind, Elle. You don't agree with his politics, but maybe outside of politics, he's a nice person.

"Dad will be here soon." Lauren's voice caused me to jump; it seemed to echo in the otherwise empty room.

I turned to find her in a different outfit than she'd been wearing earlier in the day. She'd changed into a floral pink and light blue dress that clung to her body, showcasing curves I'd never noticed before. She'd put on a little weight since I saw her last year, and the dress allowed me to see that. She actually looked good with the extra weight, in my opinion. It filled out the dress. But I knew her mother was incredibly thin, and for most of her life, so was Lauren.

She'd always made such snide comments about other women who weren't thin, so her appearance surprised me. Her hair was down, long and flowing over her shoulders in soft waves that looked professionally blown out. Her makeup was flawless. I consider myself fairly well put-together, but Lauren looked as if she'd stepped out of a magazine photo shoot.

She sighed as she walked over to the mini bar tucked away in a corner of the room. "Would you like anything?"

"No thanks."

She didn't say anything else as she poured herself a glass

of red wine - reaching nearly to the top with the glass. She swivelled and walked over to one of the chairs.

"Have a seat, stay awhile." Her words were polite, her tone offhanded. She looked at me and frowned, then looked around the room. "You didn't bring a photographer?"

"No, I'm sorry. Kelsey is actually at a Liberty High basketball game tonight."

"You think anyone cares about that sad excuse for a team? Her time would have been better spent here, with us. But I guess you'll have to do."

I bristled at her words. She was probably right; most people probably didn't care about the basketball team, but it was a tradition for us to cover their homecoming game, and I wasn't going to break tradition to satisfy a pompous politician.

"I can take photos too. It's fine."

"I'm sure you can," Lauren said dryly. She took a long swig from her glass, then placed it on the end table nearest her.

George Alexander Holt the Third entered, and it was like the air had been sucked right out of the room. He was at least 6'5, a towering presence just like his father. He looked like a younger version of his dad with sandy blonde hair and eyes that were so blue, they almost looked white. He was a handsome man if you didn't mind the perpetual look of condescension on his face. I don't think I'd ever seen him smile, not once.

He wore a black suit with a black tie, almost like he was dressed for a funeral. It was how he dressed. Always dark colors. Almost always black. Always designer.

"Oh, the prodigal son decides to grace us with his presence," Lauren muttered.

"How many glasses of wine have you had?" her brother, who went by Alex, asked in an equally dry tone.

"Just two," she answered innocently.

If the first was anything like the second, well, I could see why she might be acting a little strangely. But I kept my mouth shut. It was none of my business, and in a way, I was seeing them in their true form - as Lauren had wanted. Of course, something had changed since earlier in the day when she insisted I come over. I doubted she would have wanted me to witness this.

Alex went to the bar himself. He didn't offer me a drink. He hadn't even acknowledged my existence.

"Dad will be here shortly, and Mom is just freshening up," he said.

Lauren elaborated. "Daddy had an important meeting." She took another big drink, downing about half the glass before slamming it down on the table.

Elizabeth Holt made her presence known, as if the clink of the glass had summoned her, and it was no surprise that she had done her best to make it grand.

She swished into the room with a raspy, "Hello, darlings."

I couldn't contain the eye roll, but I did my best to hide my face from her.

Her gown was long and flowing, like something someone would wear to the Oscars, not around the house when trying to appear normal. It was Tiffany blue with crystals encrusted at the top. A matching light blue shawl covered her otherwise bare shoulders.

Elizabeth was nearing seventy but would deny it if you asked. She'd had work done to try and defy aging, but it just made her look plastic. She seemed to have no facial expressions except for perpetually startled. Her hair was colored blonde, the same as her daughter. It was long, but she always kept it pulled up , in a braided crown around her head today.

She strode to me, taking my hand in her pale, delicate ones and smiling down at me. I stood up, but she still towered over me. Like Lauren, Elizabeth was tall and thin. I wasn't short by any means, but around these people, I felt like a child.

"Ms. Schaeffer, it's such a pleasure to have you in our home," she purred. "I've always supported the free press and respect our hard-working journalists who don't get paid nearly enough. It's a thankless job."

Her comments were also way over-the-top, but at least she was being civil to me. Unlike her two spoiled children.

"Thank you, Mrs. Holt. It's a pleasure to be here. Your home is lovely."

Her smile widened as she waved her arms out, as if showing me the place for the first time. "Why thank you. I take great pride in my home. Maybe later I can give you a grand tour."

I'd hate that, I thought. "I'd love that." I smiled even though it hurt.

Elizabeth made herself a drink as well - red wine, like Lauren, but only an average amount. She glided to the sofa, and as she passed by Lauren, there was a look between them. A frown of sorts. But it passed as quickly as I'd noticed it and Elizabeth was her smiling, happy self.

"Sorry I'm late," a booming, male voice called from outside of the room.

I recognized it instantly. My hackles were raised on instinct alone.

I stood again to greet the patriarch of the family - George Holt the Second. He preferred that over being called junior, and I had a feeling that it had a lot to do with him thinking of his family like royalty. George the Second sounded like a king. George Junior didn't.

George entered the room, and Alex and Elizabeth stood. Lauren remained sitting, staring off into space as if her father hadn't just entered the room. She reminded me of a petulant child, not the thirty-six-year-old woman I knew her to be.

George purposefully moved closer to me and gave my hand a firm shake. Like his son, his eyes were nearly white, and when they stared directly at you, it was like having ice water shot through your veins. It was hard not to shiver, even in the middle of summer. His sandy blonde hair was long gone, replaced by a head of grey and white.

"Ms. Schaeffer."

"Mr. Holt."

Neither of us said it was a pleasure to see each other because the feeling between us was mutual. I didn't make his run in politics easy, and if he thought I would start now, he was wrong.

He took a seat next to his wife, and Alex sat on the other side of them, on the opposite side of Lauren. The picture of the perfect American family. But I hadn't been there half an hour and I already knew they were as dysfunctional as any other - if not more so. I found that money didn't prevent dysfunction; it often heightened it. You were just able to cover it up with fancy curtains and nice cars. You could throw money at almost any problem in the hopes of getting rid of it.

Except for me. I couldn't be bought. George Holt discovered that himself a year ago, prior to his run, when he'd offered me a large sum of money to essentially work for him and only write what he wanted me to write.

I hadn't trusted him before, but after that meeting, I despised him.

And clearly, he despised me as well.

"So where should we begin?" Elizabeth asked. "Do you have any questions for us? It's a unique chance to talk to his family, as well as the man himself." She beamed proudly, and George put a hand on her thigh, giving it a squeeze. That was the most affection I'd seen between the two of them. I'd thought they didn't touch.

"Of course. I'd love to talk to your children about their childhood and—"

"I don't think that will be necessary," George said.

I looked at Lauren. "Okay, well, Lauren wanted me to write about your family life, since I did the same for your competition. I thought—"

Alex cleared his throat and interrupted me. "My father was a good father. We never wanted for anything, and not just when it came to material objects. He was always there, supporting our endeavours. Like when I played baseball in high school. I knew I could count on my father to be at every game. Even though he was working all over the country, he would always find a way to be in the stands."

Lauren muttered something under her breath that sounded a whole lot like "Bullshit."

"Excuse me, Lauren?" I asked.

"Nothing." She took another drink from the wine glass, finishing it. She got up and returned to the bar, but her mom shot her a look.

"Lauren, do you really think that's necessary?"

Lauren didn't respond. She continued pouring herself another glass. Completely full, just like the first one. She shook the bottle and poured the last of the wine into her glass.

"Okay, well, I'd love to hear more about those baseball games," I said, returning my attention to the others. "George, how did you make it to all those games? You were a busy developer, building resorts all over the world. How did you find time to always come back for the games?"

George shrugged. "When something is important to you, you make it a priority. It's as simple as that."

Lauren returned to her seat and rolled her eyes. I really,

really wanted to hear what she had to say. "Lauren, do you have any experiences like that? Where your father made you a priority?"

Lauren snorted but covered her mouth when she realized what she'd done. Before she could answer, George pulled my attention back to him. "That article you wrote about Jeremiah…you do realize that it's not completely accurate."

"Oh?" I cocked my eyebrow. "And how was it not accurate?"

"Well, you said that he took over as mayor because he loves the town of Liberty, that he did it for the people."

"And you don't believe that?"

"No. He took over the position out of obligation. Because his father died suddenly, he was in mourning, and he wanted to make his father proud. Noble reasons, sure, but his heart clearly isn't in it. He has no experience in politics, and no desire to be there. It's why the books are such a mess right now and—"

"Excuse me, the financials were handled by the treasurer," I said, narrowing my gaze. "And they weren't a mess. There are questions that have been brought up regarding some of the funding going in and out, but I'm sure that will be cleared shortly."

"Ah, yes, your bias comes out again," George said with a chuckle.

"Excuse me?"

"We all know you have close ties to Jeremiah. He was your father's best friend," George revealed, his smile turning into a snarl that appeared almost predatory.

"I thought this was supposed to be an interview with your family to show the world what kind of man you are outside of politics. So far, you're only talking about Jeremiah."

"Well, maybe we do need to talk about Jeremiah. Considering the treasurer is dead and—"

"James is dead?" Lauren piped up. She suddenly looked very serious, sitting up straight.

James and Lauren had dated on and off a while back. I knew few details, they'd kept their relationship private, but from the look on her face, this news had hit her hard. She stared at her father, waiting for him to answer.

He didn't even acknowledge his daughter or her pain.

I felt bad for Lauren, and that wasn't something I thought I'd ever say.

"I'm not sure where you heard this news since it's not been made public. And we don't know all the facts of the case yet."

"The facts will be out there before long. And you'll see. Jeremiah isn't the man you've made him out to be."

My heart tightened in my chest. I needed to keep my composure, had to remain professional. The Holts were influential people, and this was my job. Even if it appeared that George was pushing my buttons intentionally. I couldn't understand why - except, maybe he was hoping to distract me from the drama happening in front of my eyes.

"Can we get back to talking about your family, please?"

"I think we're done here, unless Alex has more to add."

"What if I have something to add, Dad?" Lauren said, addressing her father as if his name was poison on her tongue.

"You're drunk, Lauren. And frankly, you're the reason I want to cut this short. You're an embarrassment right now."

"Right now? Don't sugarcoat it, Daddy Dearest. We both know I constantly embarrass you just by existing and being myself."

I stared at the two of them, as if waiting for a bomb to drop. I should have taken their snipes as my cue to leave, but I couldn't bring myself to stand up.

Elizabeth took it upon herself to help me. "It was a pleasure, Ms. Schaeffer, I'm so sorry about my daughter," she said. "We really should reschedule when she's feeling a bit better." She crossed the distance from the couch over to me, taking my hand in hers and helping me to stand. "Alex, can you fetch Benjamin to escort Ms. Schaeffer out?"

"I can see myself out."

"No, dear, I insist." Something about the way she said it made me think they did not want me alone in the house. She held my hand tightly, as if not willing to let it go until I was escorted by another member of her trusted family or their help.

The butler from earlier came into the room quietly.

"Benjamin, please, see her out." Elizabeth dropped my hand.

He gestured to the door, offering to allow me to precede him. I headed to the front of the house, and he was on my heels. He wouldn't let me out of his sight until I was well on my way out of there.

When we stepped out on the porch, Benjamin frowned. A man was climbing out of a black Jaguar. I knew the car; it belonged to Lauren.

"Excuse me," Benjamin said, going over to the other man. "She's not fit to drive," he hissed to the man who'd climbed out of the car.

"She called for the car herself, and we can't tell her no," the other man said. "What am I supposed to do?"

I thought Benjamin might say he'd handle it, but he just frowned. I decided I'd had enough waiting, so I walked to my car, passing by the Jaguar. My eyes fell on her license plate and I rolled my eyes so hard, I feared they might get stuck in the back of my head.

RenRox.

Ren was what I'd heard Alex call Lauren when we were younger. Perhaps at one point they'd been close enough for nicknames, before Lauren became an alcoholic and Alex an insufferable douchebag.

Benjamin rushed to my side, likely making sure I didn't touch the Jag. He held the door to my Toyota open as if it was the door to a more expensive vehicle. Had to give him props for that. At least he wasn't judging me for my choice in cars.

"Drive safely," he said stiffly.

"Thanks, Benjamin."

He froze, his eyes blinking in surprise as if he hadn't heard me right. Even though I'd used his own name, he still seemed shocked.

Then he smiled at me as he closed my car door, nodding at me as I drove off.

JEREMIAH

FBI Agent Thomas Dickinson hadn't said much since he'd walked into the room. If he thought long silences would get me to tell him something new, he was wrong. Not only was there nothing for me to tell him, I was no stranger to sitting in silence.

I could sit there all damned day without saying a word.

I stared at the tepid coffee someone had brought for me. It wasn't even room temperature and tasted like dirty water. There was no cream or sugar either, not that I usually took either, but the coffee needed something. Some flavor would have been nice.

Dickinson took a sip from his own coffee before opening the file in front of him and passed it to me.

The detective was around my age, maybe a bit older. His hair had probably been dark at one point, but what was left was now all grey. Most of it was thinning out, which he tried to cover up, but there was just too little hair to do that. He wasn't large enough to be physically intimidating, but I could imagine that his cold, patient stare was enough to make most people sweat under its scrutiny.

I glanced down at the file, but my lawyer snatched it away. Samuel Baker was a friend of mine since we'd gone to high school together. He also happened to be one of the best lawyers in Utah.

Sam frowned, the lines in his forehead deepening. He was the same age as me, but he looked older. A life filled with stress would do that to you. Give it a few more years, and chances are that the mayor's office and single fatherhood would do the same to me.

Sam flipped through the file, shaking his head, then passed it back to the agent. I had no idea what was in it.

"Even if the body found was James, there's no proof he was murdered. The autopsy report hasn't come in yet, and it'll likely be inconclusive."

"They're analyzing his dental records now. We'll know for sure soon." The agent closed the books. "And do you really think he died of natural causes?"

Dickinson watched me closely. I remained quiet. Sam had urged me silence throughout the interview. He answered for me. "Natural causes? Probably not. But suicide? Very likely."

The detective snorted. "Right. That would be pretty convenient for your client, wouldn't it? If the key whistle-blower offed himself by driving himself into that lake."

"There are many reasons he might have taken his own life, Agent Dickinson. And until you have something substantial, you can't hold my client. We are free to leave."

"Maybe we don't have anything substantial about his death, yet. But as you know, the burden of proof for financial crimes is far less than that for murder."

"And you still don't meet that," Sam said with a shrug. He picked up his briefcase and motioned for me to stand.

"We will soon. It would benefit your client to talk, tell us where he was the night of James' disappearance."

"I was at home with my daughters," I said, speaking before Sam could stop me.

"And your daughters can't collaborate, can they?"

"They're only two months old, so no."

"How convenient. How about their mother, would she be able to—"

"Their mother isn't in the picture," I snapped. "But I was at home with them. As I am every night."

"You do realize that won't hold up in court, right?"

"And you realize," Sam interrupted, "that you don't have enough evidence to even take him to court. Have a good day."

Sam grabbed my arm, and the two of us left the interrogation room. I was shaking, but not from fear. My fists were balled up at my sides. I wanted to punch something. But I held it together.

"Follow me to my office. We need to talk," Sam instructed.

We left the police station and headed for the parking lot. I climbed into my truck and Sam pulled up next to me in his BMW. He waved and drove by, and I pulled out behind him. Liberty wasn't that big of a town, so it only took five minutes to get to Sam's office.

He hurried me inside, and the expression on his face worried me a bit. But he didn't say anything until we were behind closed doors.

"I'm worried, Jeremiah," he said softly, steeping his fingers in front of his face.

"About what?" I asked. "You said yourself, they don't have enough evidence to go to trial."

"Not for the murder case, no, but the financials...well, they do look bad. This is big enough to get the feds involved. Is there anything you need to tell me?"

"Of course not. I wasn't taking bribes or paying anyone off."

Sam studied me for a moment, then nodded. "I know. I know you're not the type of man to do that, but we need to go over everything, make sure there's nothing they can question in your personal finances as well."

My heart stopped. "Like what?"

"Like money that can't be accounted for, both in and out." I stared at Sam, and his frown became a scowl. "Jesus, Jeremiah, what's that face for? Are you hiding something?"

"No, I mean—yes, but it's not what you think. I've agreed to keep the identity of the mother of my children private. We have an arrangement."

"Like a surrogacy?" he asked, raising his eyebrows.

I thought for a moment. "Sort of. But not completely. I covered all her medical bills and living costs while she was pregnant, and even after the babies were born for a bit. She needed my help."

"That's understandable," he commented. "We'd just bring her in and—"

"No, we can't. Like I said, she wants to remain anonymous."

"Jeremiah, we might need her."

I thought long and hard about this. She had reasons for not coming forward, reasons we both wanted her to remain a secret, none of which I could explain without giving her away.

"I don't think it's relevant. It shouldn't come up. They can see that the money is going to someone who's not one of the developers I'm accused of working with. She's not connected to them at all."

"That's good, and maybe it won't even come up. But if it does…"

"We'll deal with that when the time comes."

Sam remained quiet. "You know, if they take you to court for the bribery and money laundering charges, they don't need much to convince a jury that you're guilty. You could face jail time. Have you thought about what would happen to your daughters if that happened?"

I stared past him at the wall, knowing he was right. "I don't know. I'll figure it out."

Another reason they may have been better off had I put them up for adoption, I thought. No, don't think like that. You've done nothing wrong. Nothing illegal. The truth will come out. It has to.

Your daughters need you.

They have no one else.

"Is there anyone who can vouch for you the night of James' disappearance? Anyone at all? Even a cashier at a grocery store or a friend you might have called?"

I shook my head. "I don't see many people. I have my hands full with the twins, Sam. I don't have time for a social life, and I have my groceries delivered."

"Well, did you have any groceries delivered the night of his disappearance?"

"No, afraid not."

"Damn."

"But there's no way they can link me to his disappearance. I was nowhere near James' home. I never have a reason to go into that part of town. They won't find any of my DNA there, nothing. Because I wasn't there. And it's innocent until proven guilty, right?"

"It's supposed to be," Sam muttered skeptically.

"Sam, you're supposed to be more confident than this. I'm innocent."

Sam just stared at me, his brown eyes searching for the words. "I believe you, Jeremiah, but like I said, things don't look so good. We need an explanation for the money being moved around in the city's financials, and we need an explanation for James' death. We need *something*, and so far, we have nothing."

"We have the fact that I'm innocent. Isn't that enough?"

"I hope so, Jeremiah. God, I hope so."

Ooo000ooo

"I'm sorry," I said as I pushed open the door to Little Cubs. "Another emergency."

Piper was sitting in the front with my girls in the carseats I had dropped them off in earlier that day. The daycare closed forty-five minutes before I pushed through the door. I had dropped them off so suddenly when Sam had called and told me I needed to come into the police station for questioning or they'd be sending officers to my door. It had all happened so fast, and I had been kept longer than I had planned.

Piper smiled at me, holding a bottle to each girl's mouths. She was feeding them at the same time and made it look easy. Why didn't I think about using their carseats or another carrier to feed them? One bottle in each hand. I had so much to learn.

"It's alright. I decided to feed them since it's about dinner time."

"Yes, of course," I said, running a hand across my brow. It was cold and the ground was covered with snow outside, but I had worked up a sweat rushing to get to my girls. The stress didn't help, of course. "How are they doing?"

"They're doing well, Jeremiah. You've got nothing to worry about. They're almost done, just give it one second."

I plopped down on the floor beside her, sitting nearest to Grace. She had a few drinks left in the bottle, not much at all. I'd given Piper plenty of formula to have on hand in case of something like this. I wished I hadn't had to use it, or her, at all. It made me feel like a failure that I almost missed feeding time for my daughters.

"Jeremiah, it's normal to feel this way."

"Feel what way?"

She cocked her head to the side and chuckled. "That you're a failure since you can't do everything yourself. My mom had always said that it takes a village to raise children. You can't do it alone. And you're very much alone, with not one, but two babies."

"I know, but this stuff that's going on—it's not normal."

"It's also not your fault."

It was nice that Piper believed in my innocence. I wasn't as close to her as I was others in town, so knowing that she believed me meant a lot. But she also didn't know everything. No one did yet. When the news broke about James' death, that might sway some opinions.

"All done," Piper said, holding up the empty bottles.

"Thank you for staying late."

"It happens, Jeremiah. In this field, it happens more often than you'd realize. Parents are often pulled in so many directions and sometimes they're late. But you're here now, and that's all that matters."

She rose from the floor and again offered to help me to my car.

"I've got it," I said, not wanting to bother her further. She had already stayed late; she didn't need to do anything more for me. I could easily carry both carseats.

I covered them with their little blankets, careful to hold the blankets away from their faces and making sure they were nice and cozy as I carried them out the door into the dark parking lot. The streetlights illuminated the lot, and the snow even made it look brighter than it was, but it was still fairly late in the evening, and the darkness around me reminded me of that fact.

I was the only vehicle in the Little Cubs parking lot besides Piper's. The last parent to pick up his kids. I didn't want to continue down that path; I didn't want this to become a common thing.

I buckled the girls into the backseat and blasted the heat in the truck as we drove off, headed for home.

"I'm so sorry," I said, speaking to the babies, who had no idea what I was saying. "I don't want to be this type of father, and I promise you I'll be better."

I made the pledge to them knowing that even if they couldn't understand it, I did. I knew what I was promising, and I'd never willingly break a promise to anyone, especially family.

Especially my daughters.

A lump formed in my throat as I thought about the possibility that I could end up in prison. I wouldn't be able to keep my promise then.

ELLE

W*histleblower Believed to be Dead, Mayor Called in for Questioning*

Lucy's article hit my desk prior to printing early the next morning. She took the lead since I felt like maybe I was too close to all of it. I didn't want to be accused of bias.

As I read the article, I knew it had been the right decision.

Jesus, Jeremiah. What's going on here?

James Fitzhenry was believed to have been in the car found at the bottom of the lake. It was James' car, and while the remains were pretty hard to identify in their current state, he was behind the wheel. He was missing. And his wallet had been found at the bottom of the lake too - with his ID in it.

The whistleblower who talked about Jeremiah taking bribes was likely dead. Sure, it could have been suicide, which wasn't ruled out yet. But there was no indication that James was suicidal - especially since he'd agreed to work with prosecution regarding Jeremiah's corruption and there was no note. He'd just bought the BMW found at the bottom of the lake not even a month prior. He'd also bought a new house and had booked a vacation to Tahiti next month.

Not that things couldn't have gotten really bad at the last minute, but those weren't the actions of someone who didn't have a plan for the future. Which only made people question what was happening even more than before.

I closed my laptop, my eyes burning from staring at the screen for too long. I'd read and re-read the damned thing, looking for some flaw, something I could argue with and tell her she was wrong, that it couldn't go to print. Because I wanted to believe it was wrong.

I wanted to believe Jeremiah was innocent.

Maybe everyone was right. I was too close to it.

I closed my aching eyes and leaned back in the chair, rubbing my temples.

"Please don't tell my dad," I begged, my voice slurring as I spoke. *"He'll kill me."*

Jeremiah sat behind the driver's seat of his truck with a stoic look, staring straight ahead. "Elle, he's going to notice."

"Why? I can hide it," I giggled like a little girl, and once I started, I couldn't stop. Even I knew I was too drunk to hide it from anyone.

Jeremiah side-eyed me. I stopped laughing. That one look was enough to straighten me up, to almost sober me up. But not quite.

"What should I do?"

"You should walk in that door and tell him you're sorry and that it won't happen again. And you better mean it, because you're too young to fuck up your life like this."

"It was one party." I rolled my eyes. "I've never been drunk before."

"Yes, but that's how it starts. One party becomes another, and then another. I'm just grateful you didn't get behind the wheel of your car."

I had called him. I was smart enough to know I couldn't drive. I could hardly walk. I knew if I called my dad, he'd scream at me the entire drive home. But Jeremiah would be more reasonable. He always seemed to be the most reasonable man I'd ever met. He was so easy to talk to, so understanding.

Even when he was angry, he was so handsome. His face was utter perfection. Some people might have thought he was too old, and he was technically too old for me - I was only sixteen. But I had a crush on him. It wasn't just his good looks, though; it was also his kindness, the goodness I saw inside him. The fact that he was always there for me when I needed him to be.

Jeremiah's truck lurched forward and stopped. I faced the front windshield, surprised to see that we were at my house already.

I let out an audible groan. "Can we go to the diner? Get me some coffee first?"

"No," Jeremiah said sternly, undoing his seatbelt. "I'm not going to lie to your father, and neither are you. He's a good man, Elle. He only wants what's best for you."

I rolled my eyes, but inwardly, I knew he was right. My father was a good man; he was just a bit too strict sometimes. If he could have put a tracker on me to know where I was at every minute of the day, I'm sure he would have.

I stayed in the car until Jeremiah walked around and opened my door. "Come on."

My stomach roiled, partially from alcohol, partially from the nerves. I stared into Jeremiah's eyes, begging him to let me wait a bit longer. But he took my hand and helped me from the car, steadying me on my feet as I wobbled.

He walked me to the front door.

He stayed with me.

We walked into the house together, and my father was already on his feet and at the door when we stepped inside.

"Elle? Where were you?" He looked at Jeremiah. "What's going on?"

"She needs to tell you," Jeremiah said. "Just remember that she

called me for help instead of doing something that could have made things far worse."

Dad's eyes turned to me, anger in them. But not as much as I thought. No, there was an entirely different emotion in his eyes.

Disappointment.

And that hurt far more than him being angry at me.

"Elle?"

"Daddy, I'm sorry," I mumbled, slurring my words. My legs wobbled, and Jeremiah was there to help hold me up. He was my rock. "There was this boy, Shane, and he was having a party and—"

"I thought you went to Josie's," Dad said, his eyes narrowing.

"I—I lied," I admitted. "Josie is out of town visiting family."

Dad's fists balled up at his sides, and I didn't need to finish. He knew.

"Just remember, Carl, she could have driven home drunk. She called me. She did the right thing, even if she fucked up. We need to make sure she knows she can come to us when she's in trouble."

My eyes filled with tears. I didn't hear the rest of what Jeremiah said, but he didn't mention what else had happened - how Shane Wilson had led me to his room and tried to have sex with me. I didn't want to; I fought him. As soon as I got out of his bedroom, I dialed Jeremiah in tears.

I felt safe calling him.

I felt like not only would he not get me in trouble, he would help me.

My father would have helped me too, of course, but I didn't feel comfortable calling him. I knew I'd get a lecture, and at that moment, I didn't need a lecture. I knew I'd fucked up. I just wanted to go home and get into my own bed, where it was safe and there weren't pervy boys trying to take my clothes off against my will.

The buzzing of my phone pulled me out of the memory. My

heart raced as I tried to remember where I was and that I was no longer a scared sixteen-year-old girl in need of help. I picked up the phone, and saw it was Josie.

"Hello," I croaked.

"Are you alright?" my best friend asked.

"Just tired...it's been a long day," I said, rubbing my eyes. "What's up?"

"I was wondering if you wanted to grab a drink?" Josie asked.

God, did I...but I knew there was something else I needed to do instead. "I'm sorry, but I just want to go home. Like I said, long day, and I have one hell of a headache."

"I'm sorry," she sympathized. "Want me to bring you anything?"

"No thanks, but let's have drinks soon, alright?"

"Of course, Elle," Josie said. "Feel better."

I hung up, feeling bad for not meeting my friend, but I needed to help Jeremiah. I dialed his number, and it rang so many times, I thought I'd get voicemail. But Jeremiah's voice came from the other end of the line.

"Elle?"

"Yeah, it's me," I said, knowing full well I sounded weak and pathetic. I felt pretty weak, but I couldn't go home and forget about all this. I needed to do something. "Can we talk?"

"About what?" Jeremiah sounded guarded.

"About what I can do to help you."

He was quiet for a long time before saying. "Elle, there's nothing—"

"No, listen to me, Jeremiah. I know you're innocent. There's no way you could do the things you're being accused of," I insisted. "And I've got skills, I know how to dig deep for information. I can help you."

"You don't need to get involved in my business, Elle. As much as I appreciate it—"

"Think of the girls," I reminded him. "Think about them. If you go to prison, who will take care of them? Their mother? Is she even around?" He was silent for a long time. "Jeremiah?"

"Yes." He sounded annoyed. "I'm here. I'm just…I can't let you get involved in this."

"You didn't have to get involved with my problems growing up, but you always did. You always helped me. Let me repay the favor. If not for you, then for the girls. Let me do this for them."

I didn't give him a chance to argue with me. I hung up the phone, packed up my computer, and grabbed my things. I locked the office, knowing full well that when I came back the next morning, all hell would break loose over Lucy's article.

I needed to be prepared for anything. But that was tomorrow.

Tonight, it was all about trying to help clear Jeremiah's name.

JEREMIAH

"Dammit, Elle," I muttered under my breath. I had half a mind not to answer the door, but I knew she would stand out there all night, knocking and calling out my name. She was as hard-headed as her dad had been.

I put Amelia down in the pack and play in the living room next to her sister. Neither baby was sleeping - they were both fighting it, even though it was obvious they were tired. They had been cranky all evening, their little eyes trying to close, but they kept on fighting for some reason. Every time I thought one of them was about to doze off, the other would start crying and wake her sister. They were feeding off each other, and likely feeding off my stress.

Why did I think I could be a single father? I suck at this, I thought, as the two babies cried and squirmed. I wanted to hold them both, snuggle them close and tell them it would all be okay. But I wasn't sure if it would be and didn't want to cause them more stress with my own discomfort.

"Jeremiah, I know you're in there. I hear those babies," Elle called loudly, punctuating her words with more knocks.

I sighed and headed for the door. I swung it open, and

without an invitation, Elle walked inside, her laptop bag in one hand, her Michael Kors bag in the other.

"Let me at 'em," she said with a determined smile and a teasing chuckle. She dropped the bags on the floor and walked to the babies, picking up the loudest of the two, Amelia, and cradling her.

"Shh, sweet girl," she whispered, rocking her and kissing the top of her head. Amelia quieted within a few seconds.

Damn, she was good.

I walked over and picked up Grace, who was whimpering but no longer crying. Once Elle had stepped into the room, the stressful energy vanished. It was like she re-set everything just by walking in a room.

I was jealous.

As if she read my mind, she said, "You're too stressed. You need to relax, Jeremiah."

"You keep telling me that, but it's easier said than done," I grumbled.

"How can anyone be stressed around these sweeties?" Elle said, running her hand over Amelia's head and through her silky hair. The baby stared up at her with curiosity.

"You're just so good with them," I murmured. "You'll make a great mother one day." Elle visibly flinched as if my words had been a fist coming at her. "What? Did I say something wrong?"

"No, it's just..." Elle nibbled her lower lip and refused to meet my gaze. "Well, I've always wanted to be a mother, but I fear it may not be in the cards for me. It's a touchy subject."

"Oh, I'm sorry," I said. "I had no idea—I mean, I don't know what your situation is, but there's always adoption and..." Elle looked at me and I said, "Sorry. I should change the subject now."

Grace's little eyes began to close, and Amelia was already asleep in Elle's arms. Just like that.

"No, it's fine. It's just, I'm not sure if I'll meet the right guy, and if I do, either my career or the children will have to suffer. I'm not sure I can do both, not with how much I work."

"I understand."

Elle's face fell, but she noticed Amelia asleep in her arms and a smile appeared on her face. "At least I can be a part of their life. You have no idea how much this means to me."

"Well, you're always welcome to come over and help. God knows I need it."

"Don't worry, I'll always be around to help. You'll never have to ask me twice to watch these little angels. Should we put them to bed in the nursery?"

"Yes, follow me," I said, lowering my voice since Grace had just dozed off.

Elle followed me into the nursery, and we carefully put the babies down. Quietly, we snuck out of the room, and once we were back in the living room, I laughed quietly.

"You have no idea how long I've been trying to do that."

"Have you had a chance to eat?" she asked.

It seemed like an odd question, but I hadn't had a chance to have dinner yet. "No, afraid not. You hungry?"

She nodded. "Yeah, but I was more worried about you. You've got a lot going on. Let me make you dinner?"

I was taken aback by her offer. No one had ever come into my home and offered to make me dinner. I scratched my beard. "Not sure if there's much to work with."

"That's okay. I'm good at improvising," she said with a shrug, heading to the kitchen before I could stop her.

She kept calling my daughter's angels, but I had to wonder if she was one too.

Her hips swished as she hustled down the hallway, and my gaze fell to her ass. I couldn't help it, though as soon as I realized what I was doing, I scolded myself.

It was hard to imagine she was the same little girl I helped Carl with all those years ago. She was no longer a precocious child; she was a woman - and a beautiful one at that. Both inside and out.

She'll make a very lucky man very happy one day, I thought. If only I could find someone like her. Someone who loved my girls as much as she already did, who was as good with them as she was. Someone with a heart as big as hers.

I shook my head at myself. I shouldn't be holding my best friend's daughter up as the ideal woman for me, but it was true.

I needed to find me someone like Elle, but closer to my own age.

I followed her into the kitchen, and she was bent over, digging through one of the cabinets near the floor. Her skirt had risen, and I caught a glimpse of pink panties. My cheeks turned about as pink as the lacy fabric, and I had to adjust myself in my pants, turning away from her as I cleared my throat, announcing my presence.

"Where do you keep your skillets?" she asked, oblivious to the fact that I had caught a glimpse of her underwear.

"Uhh, check the dishwasher."

"You're not supposed to put those in the dishwasher!"

I heard the cabinet close, and it felt safe to turn around. After all, it would look pretty silly to be staring at a wall instead of looking at the person I was speaking to.

She was standing up, thankfully, and shooting me a disappointed look.

"What? I've been busy, I didn't even think about it," I defended. "I don't always have time to breathe, much less wash dishes."

Her frown disappeared, and a more sympathetic look replaced it. "I'm sorry, I should come over and help you more."

"No, you shouldn't. I'm a grown man and can take care of myself."

"You're also a single dad to two infants. It doesn't make you less of a man to ask for help, Jeremiah." She pulled out the skillet and shook her head but didn't say anything more about it. She walked over to the fridge and pulled out something. "Make a shopping list, and I can pick things up for you tomorrow after work and drop them off."

"I can go to the grocery store myself."

"I have to take Mom a few times a week anyway. It's no bother, really."

"It's alright. I can handle the shopping, Elle. You just caught me in a bad time." *Yeah, because I've been spending so much of my time being questioned about crimes I didn't commit.*

She didn't argue with me. I heard sizzling from the frying pan, and the smell of bacon hit my nose. I hadn't really been hungry before that moment, but my stomach growled at the smell.

"Breakfast for dinner will have to do," she announced. "Bacon and eggs, no biscuits or anything. Does that sound alright?"

"Yeah, it sounds perfect. Better than what I would have had on my own."

She looked over her shoulder, and I hated that look of pity on her face. I hated that she felt sorry for me.

"Would you like a beer?" I asked, moving to the fridge.

"Sure, but you know I don't drink much."

"I know," I said with a chuckle. "Ever since that lecture I gave you that night."

She blushed cutely and turned away from me, focusing on the food. I handed her a beer and wandered to the kitchen table, where I popped open mine and took a big swig.

Elle finished cooking fairly quickly, plating the food and bringing it over to the table.

"My dad always loved breakfast for dinner," she said, chuckling. "He always said, food is food, it doesn't matter—"

I finished her sentence for her— "what time of day it is. It all goes down the same."

"Yes! God, I miss his French toast. I don't know what he did, but he did something that made it taste better than any I've had before."

"Nutmeg and cinnamon in the egg mixture," I said, taking a big bite. The food tasted delicious; the bacon was crispy but not overdone, just the way I liked it. Just the way Elle liked it too. We'd had breakfast together many times, when I'd stop by for a visit at her dad's place early on the weekends.

"That's the secret?" she asked, chuckling and shaking her head. "All these years, I had no idea."

"Yep. He loved nutmeg. He put that stuff on everything."

Elle took a bite of bacon and seemed to be lost in thought. "Huh, I guess he did. I never noticed. Sometimes it feels like I didn't even know him at all."

"A child will never know everything about their parents."

"Yeah, I know, but I wish I could."

There was a long silence as we ate the rest of our food.

"Does it ever feel like you never really know anyone?" she asked, staring down at her empty plate.

"I think so. We may not know everything about someone. We may not know that nutmeg is their favorite spice or everything they did in the past, but the things that matter? Yes, it's possible."

"And what matters? Who decides what's important and what's not when knowing someone?"

I shrugged and licked my fork clean, placing it on the plate. "You sure do ask hard questions, Elle. Always did."

She grinned at me. "Some things don't change."

I thought about her question for a long while, but she ended up answering it on her own.

"You know, what matters is up to the individual, but I think we can all agree that some parts of a person are more important than others. Like, can you trust them? Are they the type of person who will be there for you when you need them?"

"It almost feels like you're going somewhere with this. Like it's relevant to everything that's going on."

"I am," she said with a cheeky grin. "Because people keep asking me how I can still believe your innocent, even as the evidence continues to stack up. It's because I know the things that matter about you. I know the type of person you are. And you're not someone who would accept bribes, and you're most certainly not a murderer."

She stood up and walked over to me, reaching for my plate. I grabbed her hand, intending to stop her since I should do the dishes. She'd cooked, after all.

But when I grabbed her hand, she just stopped and stared at me, her brown eyes the color of sweet bourbon, a golden tinge to them that I'd never noticed before.

Her lips were pink, and not from lipstick.

I didn't even know who made the first move, but somehow, those lips came closer and were touching mine.

So soft and warm.

Her tongue was velvety soft against my own.

Her jacket fell to the floor with a whoosh, her silk shirt brushing against my hands as I fisted the material, pulling at it.

Elle moved closer to me, climbing into my lap. Her body pressed against my erection, grinding against me. Her movements were clumsy. The chair wasn't sturdy enough for both of us. The sound of glass shattering pulled my attention from her body against mine.

And I realized what I was doing.

I jerked away from her mouth and dropped my hands. "I'm sorry, we shouldn't—"

Elle stepped back, getting to her feet. Her cheeks were no longer pink, but bright red. She wouldn't meet my gaze.

I stood up too, to find the empty plate on the floor, in pieces along with the beer bottle. "I need to clean this up," I muttered, trying to distract myself from what had just happened.

That didn't just happen. It couldn't have. I didn't just kiss my deceased best friend's daughter. I didn't just have her in my lap, grinding against my erection. The erection that I had for her.

"I think you should go," I mumbled, not looking at her.

"No," she said. Just a simple one-word response to my request.

"Excuse me?" I said, looking up in surprise.

"No, I'm not going anywhere. I came here to help you, Jeremiah, and I'm not leaving until we figure out what we're going to do."

She stood in my kitchen, her chin kicked out defiantly, hands crossed in front of her chest. Her cheeks were slowly returning to their normal color.

"Elle, we just—" I couldn't put into words what we'd just done. It still felt so wrong to me. So very wrong. I looked down at the mess on the floor, feeling it was the perfect metaphor for my life at the moment.

But then I looked back up and saw her. Her beautiful blonde hair had fallen from loose around her face, and she looked more dishevelled than I'd ever seen her before.

But God, she still looked like an angel to me. My cock twitched in my pants, aching as it pressed against my jeans.

She needed to leave. I had to get her out of there before I did something stupid.

Again.

ELLE

Jeremiah tried not to meet my gaze. He wouldn't look at me for more than a second, but he stole glances in my direction as he lowered himself to clean up the mess on the floor.

My lips felt warm and tingly, and I could still feel his mouth against mine. His tongue sliding over my own.

I'd felt his erection pressing against me when I straddled him. His hands nearly ripped off my clothes.

But then I knocked the plate off the table, and it ended so suddenly.

I cursed myself for being so clumsy.

For being so careless.

In more ways than one.

I shouldn't be kissing him; he was my dad's best friend. Yes, I'd had a crush on him for as long as I could remember, but that didn't mean it should become a reality.

Especially with everything going on.

"Here, let me help you," I mumbled, hurrying to the closet in the hallway outside of the kitchen. I grabbed the broom and dustpan, and Jeremiah took the broom from me.

I knelt, dustpan in hand.

"I've got it," he grumbled. "You should go."

"I'm not going anywhere," I retorted. "I came over to help you, and that's what I'm going to do."

"You've helped enough." He swept the mess into the dustpan I was holding. He didn't fight me about that, at least.

"We haven't figured out what we're going to do about this problem yet."

"We don't have to do it tonight."

"If not now, when? You can't continue to avoid the issue." My voice was raised. I stared up at him as he finished sweeping the glass. Once the floor was clear, I stood and walked over to the trash can to dump the mess into it.

"I'm not avoiding anything. I know I'm innocent and the truth will come out eventually." As he said those words, his voice shook. Just a bit. He wanted to believe it, he kept telling himself that, but he had some doubts.

"Yeah, because innocent people never end up behind bars," I said dryly, rolling my eyes as I turned to face him. "Spoiler alert, Jeremiah. They do. All the damned time. And I don't want you to be one of them. Your daughters need you."

He looked me dead in the eyes, and it look took my breath away. I felt like I couldn't breathe for a second, and that look alone could warm a whole house on a cold winter's night.

I wasn't aware of my feet moving forward until I was standing right in front of him. He stared down at me, towering over me. His jaw was set tight, his lips pursed as if he was trying to keep them shut.

Or keep them away from mine.

I licked my lips, remembering how surprisingly soft his had felt. For such a rough, tough man, his kiss had been gentler than I'd expected.

Filled with need, but soft and sweet at the same time.

That summed up Jeremiah perfectly, in my opinion. He was tough on the outside, but warm and gooey on the inside. And very few people got to see the gooey center of him. I was one of the lucky few.

"Elle, I have a lawyer. We can handle this without your help." His words were stern, almost like he was talking to his daughter.

"And you also have a journalist, someone with detective skills that rival the FBI's." Maybe a slight exaggeration, but oh well. I was good and I knew it. No need to water it down and pretend to be humble.

"You're so damn stubborn, do you know that?"

I cracked a smile. "Admit it, you always liked that part of me."

"Sometimes. But sometimes it's a tad bit annoying."

His face moved closer to mine; his hand was on my arm. All of it happened in a blink of an eye.

"How do you feel now?" I asked, breathless. I licked my lips again and stood on my tiptoes, trying to lift myself to his height.

He leaned down to meet me, his lips pressing into mine. He answered the question not with his words, but with his body.

He held onto my arms, backing us both up until I was pressed against the counter. Jeremiah's hungry hands pulled at my top, yanking it up over my head and disposing it onto the ground.

He grabbed my ass, lifting me off the floor and sitting me on the counter. I wrapped my legs around his waist, and he pressed against me. His erection rubbed my most sensitive parts, only the clothing separating us.

And he was making quick work of my skirt, lifting it up. I fumbled with his belt, then his zipper. I needed to free him from those jeans.

I needed to feel him against me.

Inside me.

Jeremiah's fingers rubbed against the crotch of my panties; he had to feel the wetness. He had to see how much I wanted him, how much I needed him. How much I craved him.

His fingers slipped inside my panties, circling my clit. I groaned against his mouth. "Please, Jeremiah, I need you."

He buried his fingers inside me, causing my thighs to shake from pleasure. I gripped his shirt, pulling at it - wanting it off, wanting to see him naked. But our position didn't make it easy, and I soon became lost in the sensation of his fingers stretching me, moving in and out of me.

His lips moved down to my neck, then my cleavage, dotting kisses along my flesh. Sweet, gentle kisses again, but his fingers were anything but sweet inside me. He fingered me like he had a mission in life to make me orgasm as quickly as possible, and it was working.

"Oh God," I cried out, my entire body tensing. "Oh God, Jeremiah, I'm—"

I never finished the sentence, at least not with words that made any sense. I groaned as I came, and he never let up - even as my body squirmed and flailed.

As the last wave of pleasure washed over me, I knew it wasn't enough. I needed more.

Reaching down, I slipped his pants over his hips. His boxers too. I took him in my hands, and marvelled at his thickness and length. He was bigger than I expected, though I don't know why I thought he'd be anything but well-endowed. He was a large man.

Jeremiah moved forward, and I guided him to my opening. He held my panties aside, and before I could even take a breath to prepare myself, he thrust into me. I whimpered, clinging to him for dear life as he stretched me wider than I'd been stretched before. My entire body reacted to his penetration.

"Did I hurt you?" he asked, his voice soft. He rested his forehead against mine and, stared into my eyes.

"No, not at all. It feels so good."

"Good." He began moving in and out of me, and there was so much intensity in his movements. As if he was desperate.

Each thrust seemed to reach deeper and deeper, and I was a ragdoll in his arms. I was pressed against him, my face falling forward, resting in the crook of his neck as he fucked me. There was nothing gentle in that part. He fucked me wildly and with passion, and I loved every moment of it.

My pussy spasmed around his cock, clenching and releasing as I came close to climax again. Jeremiah's breathing was ragged, his movements more desperate. Thunderous groans came from his lips.

No, not groans. Growls.

"Jeremiah, I'm close," I whimpered.

"Cum for me, Elle," he demanded.

My body exploded with pleasure as I obeyed his command, my orgasm bringing out his own. He thrust into me, one long, deep thrust, and that was it. He remained inside me, his cock pulsing as I spasmed around him.

We came together.

And it was beautiful.

Our bodies remained connected for several moments, until he slipped his cock out of me. A rush of warmth coated my thighs, and it was a beautiful, intimate feeling.

Jeremiah took my face in his hands, forcing me to stare into his eyes. I offered a sleepy smile, but his face was completely serious.

"I'm sorry," he said, his voice soft. "I shouldn't have done that."

My smile disappeared. "What do you mean? Don't be sorry. I wanted it as much as you did, Jeremiah."

"I know, but you're Carl's daughter. It's wrong." He stepped away from me, nearly tripping on his pants around his ankles. He pulled them up quickly, not looking at me as he did.

I hopped down from the counter. "Yes, but I'm not a child anymore. I'm a grown-ass woman, and I wanted that as much as you did."

Jeremiah didn't speak. He picked up my shirt and handed it to me.

I quickly, jerkily dressed. "If you think this means I'm not going to help you with the case, you're wrong. I'm still going to do that."

"It could get ugly, Elle."

"I know that. I know how these things go, and I'm willing to do whatever it takes. For both you and your girls."

Jeremiah closed his eyes and a pained expression crossed his face. He knew there was no way he would win this argument. No way. I'd do what I want.

"Can we talk about this another time, please?"

I wanted to keep pushing it, but Jeremiah looked exhausted. He looked on the verge of tears, and that's saying a lot for a man like him. I only saw him cry once in his life, and that was at my daddy's funeral.

"Sure, of course. Just know that I'm going to get to work on this as soon as possible."

He didn't answer me. He didn't even acknowledge what I'd said, but I knew he'd heard me. He just knew there was no use arguing with me.

"I'll leave for now," I whispered, knowing when Jeremiah was shutting down. If I stayed, it wouldn't matter. He claimed I was stubborn, but so was he. He would shut down and shut me out for the rest of the night; he needed his space.

I'd give him his space. He had a lot to process, as did I.

I walked toward the hallway, stopping to pick up my jacket.

"You left your other one here too."

"I can pick it up later," I said, watching him closely. He nodded. I continued walking, and Jeremiah followed me to the door.

"I'd walk you to the car, but the girls…"

"It's alright. I'm a big girl."

I thought about it for a moment and finally decided to go for it. I stood on my tiptoes and brushed my lips against his cheek.

"Talk soon, Jeremiah."

"Talk soon."

I walked out to my car, knowing Jeremiah was in the doorway, watching me. The light from his house created a path to my car. I climbed inside, and as I pulled out, I waved at him.

Once I was on the main road, the reality of what we'd done hit me hard.

I just fucked my father's best friend, who also happened to be the man of my dreams. The man I had compared every other man to for as long as I could remember, and none of them had stacked up.

"Siri, call Josie."

The phone only rang once. "Hey, feeling better?" my best friend asked over the speakerphone.

"Oh, hell yes. Girl, you have no idea."

JEREMIAH

What did I do?

I stared up at the ceiling, the sun was beginning to stream in through the curtains. I'd been lying in my bed, tossing and turning for hours. The girls would be awake soon, and I didn't get a minute of sleep.

It was going to be a long day.

Luckily, I didn't have to go into work. Not that my reasons for taking the day off were a good one - I was put on leave while they investigated the charges. While that would probably upset most normal folks, I was a little relieved. Not because I was tired from lack of sleep, but because after everything, I really just wanted to spend time at home with my girls.

Speaking of which… It started as a muffled cry, then the other joined in and it was a screaming fest.

Breakfast time.

For them, not me. I still needed to go to the store. Elle had used the last of the eggs and bacon the night before and I—

Elle.

I fucked Elle.

I mentally kicked myself again. If I could have physically done so, I would have.

Stop it, Jeremiah. Feed your girls. Go to the store. You can deal with Elle later. Add it to your list of things to do, along with trying to clear your name and not go to prison for murder.

I didn't remember walking into the kitchen, or even preparing the bottles. I was in my head but trying hard not to think too much. The kitchen reminded me of her.

Right here, on this very counter. The one you're preparing your daughter's bottles on. You fucked your best friend's daughter right here.

Had the tables been reversed and Carl was still alive when my daughters were of age, I'd have killed him.

I knew he'd have done the same if he was alive.

But he wasn't.

I dishonored him by fucking his daughter.

I cursed myself as I took the two bottles and walked toward the nursery. I was a father now, I should have known better. I should have had more self-control.

I entered the nursery to Amelia and Grace crying in harmony. You know, prior to having kids, anytime I was around crying babies, it annoyed me. Now that I had my own, it only broke my heart to hear their pitiful cries.

I'd do anything to make sure they never had to cry again.

After changing dirty diapers as quickly as possible, I took a page from Piper's playbook, putting the girls in their carriers. Then I sat down in the middle of the floor, a bottle in each hand, and fed my babies.

Elle was right about us not having food in the house, and I was running low on formula too. I needed to get to the store. I could put in a grocery delivery order, but then I remembered that made for a terrible alibi. I needed to be seen more, just in case someone else ended up dead.

Sad that I had to think about things like that, but it was true. I couldn't stay locked in my house if I wanted to prove my innocence.

Once the girl's finished, I dressed them in some warm clothes. I felt like my body was moving on autopilot. I didn't want to think too much, because every time I did, I felt guilty.

My brain kept taking me back to the night before, no matter what else I was trying to think about.

Getting out would also be a good distraction. Get my mind off things.

I drove to the only grocery store in Liberty and parked as close to the front as I could. It was cold, but not freezing. There was fresh snow on the ground from the night before, but the sun was out and already melting a lot of it.

Old snow was piled high along the parking lot, turned to grey mush, but it too was melting. We still had a few weeks of winter left, and considering we were in the mountains, I knew that the snow wasn't going anywhere for long. But at least it wasn't too cold for my girls today.

I'd finally get to use the baby carrier I bought, the one meant for two babies. They were both in the front, side-by-side and resting against my chest. It was a lot easier than dealing with two carseats in the store.

I walked in and grabbed a cart, running down my shopping list to prevent me from thinking about Elle. Dammit. Even then, I thought about her and how she offered to pick things up for me when she took her mother shopping.

No thought was exempt from reminding me about her.

I pushed the cart through the bakery and deli section and turned down the aisle for bread when I heard a familiar voice.

"I'll just grab some bagels."

My heart stopped.

I stopped.

Even though I was right by the bagels.

Pamela Schaffer turned the corner before I could bolt, and her eyes lit up when she saw me.

"Oh my God, Jeremiah! Are those the little girls Elle keeps going on and on about?" Pamela cooed, rushing toward me.

"Mom, I—"

Elle turned the corner and saw me just as her mother reached me and the girls. She was wearing dress slacks and a green, silk blouse that complemented the brown of her eyes perfectly. I knew this was her casual attire - Elle didn't really do casual, she always dressed to impress. It was the New York girl in here. Even before she moved to the big city, she was a New York socialite at heart.

"Oh, hello, Jeremiah," Elle murmured.

She wasn't usually lost for words. But even the talkative, extroverted Elle seemed not to know what to say to me. She looked down, focusing on something on the shelf as if it was the most interesting brand of bagels in the world.

"Aren't they just darling? They look just like you, too." Pamela continued cooing at the babies, oblivious to the elephant in the room, the one standing between her daughter and me.

"Elle, get your butt over here and look at them."

"I've seen them, Mom," she said.

"Oh, you have? I guess you interviewed him recently, huh?" Pamela looked up at me, and she had the same brown eyes as her daughter. She looked older than I remembered, more tired. I knew she hadn't handled Carl's death very well. She was thinner than I remembered too. "Why haven't you been over for dinner in a while? Just because Carl's gone doesn't mean you can't come visit us?"

Elle raised her eyebrows but didn't say anything.

"Uh, yeah, you're right," I said, scratching my beard. "I've been busy, and you know, I didn't want to intrude. I know you've been through a lot."

"So have you," Pamela said softly. "But we're family. Aren't we, Elle?"

"Of course," Elle agreed quickly. Then she looked up at me, her eyes reaching deep into my soul. "You really should come by sometime, Jeremiah."

I swallowed. "I'll try, but it's a bit hard with two babies."

Elle moved closer, more relaxed, and smiled down at Amelia. "How's my sweet girl?" she asked, running her fingers over the baby's down-soft hair. "Daddy finally getting some groceries, huh?"

"What are you talking about, Elle?"

"Oh, nothing," Elle said, brushing off the comment. "Just the last time I saw him, he said he needed to pick up some groceries. I offered to help, but you know Jeremiah."

"Yes, always so stubborn. Just like your dad."

And just like your daughter, but I kept that thought to myself.

"Well, I really need to get going," I stammered.

"Oh, of course, sorry to keep you. But I mean it, if you need a warm meal, Elle is one heck of a cook, and we'd be happy to have you over."

Elle smiled at me, even though it was slightly awkward. I don't think she knew how to feel about what happened.

Glad it wasn't just me.

"Thank you," I muttered, pushing the cart forward and past the two women. "I'll see what I can do."

As soon as I was out of range, I breathed a sigh of relief. Closing my eyes, I pictured her up on the counter, her legs wrapped around me.

Stop it.

She had been so wet for me from the start. I slipped right inside her. So tight. So wet. So warm.

Stop it!

My eyes popped open. *Pull yourself together, Jeremiah. You can't ignore Elle forever. You live in a small town, it was only a matter of time before you ran into her.*

But why the very next day?

She had mentioned taking her mom shopping. Why did I decide to go shopping too? Was it intentional? Hell, no. I knew better than that.

Her mother had no idea that I'd fucked her sweet, innocent daughter on my kitchen countertop.

It couldn't happen again.

Grace began to fuss, and I realized I'd been standing still for too long. I needed to get moving so I could be home before they needed changing.

I hurried through the store, only picking up what I needed - the bare minimum - and headed for the front. I scanned the lines and didn't see Elle or Pamela. I got into the shortest line and rushed through the checkout process. I prayed they'd left already.

Maybe I could avoid another awkward run-in with the two of them.

I grabbed the bags as soon as the transaction was over.

"I don't need a receipt."

I would have run out to my truck had it just been me, but I had my girls strapped to my chest. I walked as quickly as I could. When I got to the door, I thought I was in the clear.

"Jeremiah, wait."

Apparently not.

I turned, expecting to see Elle and her mother. Probably insisting I come over for dinner later. I would need a very good excuse. I loved them, they were like family, but after last night, I couldn't do it.

I couldn't bear to look Mrs. Schaeffer in the eye through dinner, knowing that I'd had my way with her daughter. I couldn't look at photos of Carl, not without feeling like a terrible friend.

Elle hurried to me, her wool jacket wrapped tightly around her. No sign of her mother. At least I could count that one blessing, however small it might be.

She waited until she was right up to me to talk and spoke in a low voice. "I may have something already. A witness saw a car outside James' house the night he disappeared."

"Elle, if it's relevant, the police will handle it."

"She told Teddy. I spoke to Teddy, and he said his hands were tied, but he'd handed the witness's name over to the FBI. The witness said no one from the feds have spoken to her yet. They aren't even looking into it."

"Even more reason to stay out of it."

She stared at me like I was crazy. "That makes no sense. If they aren't going to look into a key piece of information, someone needs to."

"Maybe it's not relevant."

She huffed, her hands on her hips. "Or maybe they just don't think it is. It could have slipped through the cracks. Either way, it won't hurt for me to talk to the woman—"

"Elle?" Pamela's voice pulled my head up. She was walking out of the store with a cart full of bags, heading right for us.

"Elle, don't—"

"So if it's no problem, I'll be by later for my jacket," Elle trilled, smiling brightly. "I can't believe I left it when I interviewed you for that article."

Pamela walked up. "Oh, you forgot your jacket?"

"Mmhmm. When I was interviewing him the other day for the article."

Pamela frowned. "You should have told me you talked to him, dear. I thought you only wrote that article based on what you knew about him."

"It slipped my mind, Mom. I'm sorry."

"It's okay, I just would have liked to join you and meet the babies, but I've met them now. So it's all good."

"I really need to get them in the truck. It's cold," I intervened. "But it was nice seeing you."

I hurried and unlocked the back door, and my hands were fumbling with the carseat. I heard the two of them say goodbye and walk away, but I kept thinking maybe Elle would come back.

Maybe her mother would too.

Maybe Pamela would find out the truth. Because I swear, the guilt had to be written all over my face.

ELLE

Violet Murphy lived by herself, and I think that was part of the reason she chose this neighborhood after her husband died years ago. It was one of the few neighborhoods inside the city limits of Liberty. It was an upper-middle class area, mostly two-story homes with small yards and within walking distance of everything that Liberty had to offer. Her house was nice - very nice, in fact - but nothing compared to the likes of the Holts or some of our more wealthy residents.

James Fitzhenry had just bought a home in the neighborhood before he disappeared. I wondered if he even had the opportunity to meet his neighbors. I didn't know the man very well, but he'd seemed nice enough. He had also been tied to Lauren Holt, so maybe he was horrible. Not that I would know.

Maybe Violet Murphy would be able to tell me.

The older woman used a walker, but she still greeted me at the door.

"Mrs. Murphy, thank you for meeting with me today," I said.

She took my hands in hers and stared into my eyes. Her glasses were as thick as coke bottles, and her eyes cloudy. "Oh, of course, dear. Always happy to help the police."

"I'm not the police, Mrs. Murphy. I—"

"Please, call me Violet."

I cleared my throat. "Sorry, Violet. As I told you over the phone, I'm a journalist and a good friend of Jeremiah Jenkins, not the police. I'm only here as a friend to Jeremiah."

"Oh, yes, that's right. Come on inside."

As I followed her down the hallway and into her living room, I noticed the window in the room had a direct view of James Fitzhenry's house and the street in front of it.

I helped Violet take a seat on the sofa before sitting across from her in a chair.

"Oh, I'm sorry, I should have offered you some tea or something to drink."

"It's fine," I assured with a smile. *What a sweet woman,* I thought. I wouldn't dare ask her to get me anything. She barely made it down the hallway.

"Can I get you anything, Violet?"

"No, it's okay, dear," she said. Then she cocked her head to the side as if trying to figure something out. "I already told the police everything I know."

"Oh, I'm not the police," I said again.

"That's right. You're the journalist. I read your paper, have every day since I moved to Liberty in 1977. But you weren't born yet, were you?"

"No, I wasn't." I chuckled.

"Yes, yes, you're far too young. And you work for the FBI?"

"No, Violet. I'm a journalist."

"That's right. My head gets jumbled sometimes."

I was beginning to see why maybe the FBI didn't take her statement seriously. Was I wasting my time?

"So what can you tell me about the night your neighbor, James Fitzhenry, disappeared?"

"Oh, he was the young man who moved in next door, right?"

"Yes, he was."

"He kept to himself. I don't think I ever talked to him. His girlfriend wasn't very nice, though." She clicked her tongue unhappily.

Okay, she's in her right mind enough to remember Lauren, so that's a plus.

She frowned. "Her car was here that night."

"Pardon?"

"Yes, her fancy schmancy panther or whatever it is she drives. It was parked out front."

Lauren had told the police she was out of the country. Some tropical island or something. I couldn't remember her exact story, but she was cleared and supposedly not in the area.

"Do you mean Jaguar?" I asked.

"Jaguar, panther, I can't keep up with the latest brands."

"Are you sure it was her car?"

"Of course I'm sure. We may be doing well financially here, but we're not that rich. Cars like that aren't usually parked outside, and she never parked on the street, which is why I found it odd."

Yeah, I did too. I couldn't imagine Lauren would park on the street, not when the house had a three-car garage and, unlike her dad, James only had one vehicle.

"You sure it was that night?"

"Positive. I was sitting here, watching *Jeopardy* when her headlights nearly blinded me. I had to get up and close the curtains and saw her car on the street."

"Did you see her get out or anything?"

"No, I closed the curtain and went back to watching TV. I'm no snoop."

"Right," I said, leaning back in the chair. Violet Murphy seemed sure of this. She saw Lauren's car, and it was parked outside the night James disappeared. Knowing the neighborhood, there was a good chance someone had security cameras. James didn't. Well, he had, but they were turned off. It was believed he hadn't set them up yet. Maybe that was true. Or maybe someone turned them off and deleted everything from them.

"Thank you for your time, Mrs. Murphy. I can see myself out."

I wasn't sure if I could make heads or tails of what she'd said. At times, she seemed to be confused. At others, she seemed to have moments of clarity. She could recount what she was doing and why it bothered her. She seemed certain it was Lauren's car parked in front of his house that particular night. But what did it mean?

Lauren and James had broken up several times over the last few years. At the time of his disappearance, she claimed that were no longer together. She'd been away for almost a year, or so she said.

But if she'd been to his home since he'd bought it, well, that changed everything.

Ooo000ooo

"Jeremiah!" I knocked on his door. "I know you're in there!"

It took him a moment, as I expected it might. He was probably feeding the girls or taking care of them in come capacity. He had his hands full.

But the door swung open and there he was, looking as exhausted as I'd ever seen him. I entered the house without saying hello before I let it all out.

"The witness saw Lauren's car outside James' house the night of the disappearance, but she's not exactly in her right mind, so I can see why the Feds might have dismissed her testimony, but Lauren insisted that she was out of the country and the neighbor had seen her there and she claimed to have been away for the last year or so and—"

"Elle—"

"And I believe her because she seemed to remember a lot of details about that night. At least what she was doing, and why she noticed and her window—"

"Elle—"

"--looks right outside onto the front of his house. But what I don't get is why would Lauren park her Jag on the street when there's a garage, unless James didn't let her park in the garage for some reason and—"

"Elle!"

Jeremiah's raised voice stopped me in my tracks. I hadn't even realized my feet continued moving, and I was in his living room. His girls were in their pack and plays, asleep. And I was going on and on, unaware of the tone of my voice.

I covered my mouth and turned on my heels, whispering. "I'm so sorry. I should have been quieter."

"It's not that," Jeremiah said, taking my arm and leading me out of the room and into the kitchen nearby. "Calm down, okay? Slow down. I couldn't make out half of what you were saying."

I took a deep breath. "Alright, so Mrs. Murphy saw Lauren's Jaguar out front of James' house that night."

"Mrs. Violet Murphy?" Jeremiah raised his eyebrows, crossing his arms in front of his chest.

"Yes."

"She's the grandmother of one of my staff, and last time I heard her Alzheimer's was so bad, they wanted to put her in a home, but the old woman is fighting it. They're trying to get power of attorney and stand a good chance at it, Elle."

"I know, but she had moments of clarity..." As I said those words, I knew he was right. I knew there was no way it would stand up in court. "But she had met Lauren, she even said she didn't like her. But Lauren told police she hadn't been in Liberty in around ten months or so, which is a lie."

"Is it?"

"I mean, Mrs. Murphy had seen her around."

Jeremiah sighed, the lines in his face growing deeper and aging him. "But you agree she's not a reliable witness, right?"

"Yes, but maybe at least some of what she's saying fits," I tried.

"Maybe? Maybe not," Jeremiah said. "It's not Lauren."

"How do you know? The jilted ex? It very well could be a coincidence—"

"It's not Lauren. Drop it, Elle." His voice was raised, his tone heated.

Almost as heated as his eyes, which hadn't moved off me.

"Jeremiah, I don't—"

Before I could continue the sentence, Jeremiah moved toward me. His lips pressed against mine, stopping me from continuing my thoughts.

I forgot everything I was thinking anyway.

All I could think about was his lips on mine.

I pulled away for a second. "What if we wake the babies?"

"We won't," he said against my lips.

I pressed my lips back to his, and he lifted me in his arms. I'm not sure what changed from the night before, what made Jeremiah react the way he was - but it didn't matter to me.

I wanted to be his.

"We shouldn't..." he whispered without pulling away.

"We're both adults, Jeremiah. I'm a grown woman, and I want this."

That was all he needed to hear. He carried me to the bedroom at the end of the hallway, kicking open the door, his mouth never leaving mine.

Everything happened so fast - he removed my clothes, ripping and tearing them off me, impatient and demanding. I did the same to him. Before long, I could stare up at him and see all of him.

He sat me on the edge of the bed and stood before me.

And he was as marvelous as I imagined him to be.

His body was a work of art, a fine, chiselled sculpture that belonged in a museum beside Michelangelo's *David*. His muscles weren't just for show, either. He worked in construction, building many of the homes in Liberty before he became mayor. I grew up watching him chop wood, cut down trees, and build things with his bare hands.

And his body was as beautiful and perfect as it was back then.

I ran my hands down his washboard abs, feeling the muscles tremble as I worked down toward his manhood. I'd felt him the night before, but this was the first time I got to see it. I couldn't even wrap my hand around him fully. I stroked him, moving my hand up and down while meeting his gaze.

If there was any doubt left in his mind, it slipped away as I stroked his cock. I could see it in his eyes. He wanted me.

Jeremiah gently removed my hand, and for a second, I thought he might be stopping me. But he dropped to his knees onto the floor. He pushed my thighs apart, burying his head between them. His fingers parted my lips, and his tongue... oh God, his tongue found just the right spot to make my entire body tremble like an earthquake.

He licked me, slow and languorously, as if he were

savoring it. As if he was enjoying it and never wanted it to end.

The feeling was mutual.

His nails bit into the flesh of my hips, holding me in place as he licked ferociously. His tongue was buried deep inside of me, tasting me from the inside out. My hands gripped the back of his head, pressing him into me. My legs were now draped over his shoulders, heels digging into his back.

"Jeremiah, yes," I whimpered. "Don't stop, please don't stop."

Not that he was giving me any indication of stopping. He was licking and fucking me with his tongue like it was his job. He knew all the right spots to hit, the rhythm to bring me right to the brink.

My nails dug into his scalp as I cried out. My orgasm hit me hard and fast, taking me by surprise. I would normally have tried to be quiet for the babies' sake, but I didn't have time to prepare.

I threw my head back and let the pleasure wash over me. I couldn't believe I was here, orgasming because of my dad's best friend's tongue. The man of my dreams.

As soon as my orgasm subsided, I pulled on his hair.

"Come up here," I said, my voice still shaky. "Now."

Jeremiah stood up, but he wasn't standing for long. I pulled him onto the bed, on top of me. Our bodies crashed together. I wrapped my legs around him, everything pressing against him. His lips met mine, and I tasted myself on him.

You'd think my orgasm would have sated me, but it did nothing but light the flame inside me. I needed more of him.

His cock rubbed against me, teasing my opening and stroking my clit. I reached down, gripped him with my hand, and guided him to where he needed to go.

Jeremiah thrust into me with a deep, satisfied groan. He buried himself inside, balls deep, with one thrust. He stayed

92 | K.C. CROWNE

that way for a second, letting our bodies get used to the sensation.

I wondered if I'd ever get used to his thickness stretching me, but the feeling of him sheathed inside me was amazing. I clenched my Kegels around me, squeezing and releasing, which brought out another lengthy groan.

"Jesus, you're going to be the death of me, Elle" he growled, before slowing rocking back and forth, moving in and out of me.

Our bodies found our own perfect rhythm. Jeremiah began moving faster, thrusting deeper and deeper and hitting all the right spots. Every thrust, I arched upward to meet him. We were in perfect harmony, and nothing had ever felt so perfect in my life.

He rested his forehead against mine and stared into my eyes. He took my hands in his, pressing them against the bed as he continued fucking me. It was so intimate. So perfect. It was like my first time all over again. Which was even more perfect, since I'd always wanted my first time to be with him.

So many emotions bubbled to the surface. I wanted to tell him I loved him, but it was too soon. *Too soon? Yes, Elle. But you've known him your entire life. Yes, but not like this.*

I'd never had sex like this before, with so much depth. So much emotion. And I saw the care in his eyes he had for me. Maybe it wasn't love in a romantic sense, yet, but he did love me.

He would always take care of me.

My pussy spasmed as another orgasm washed over me. I clung to Jeremiah, my eyes fighting to close, but I wanted to look in his eyes.

I wanted him to see what he did to me. How he made me feel.

I writhed underneath him, only held in place by his strong body. I came once, then twice, then a third time. I'd never had multiple orgasms before, but something about him kept pushing me to the edge, over and over again.

His face contorted into a look of bliss, and I knew he was close too.

"Cum inside me," I begged. Maybe I should have been more careful, maybe I should have thought about what I was asking, but in the moment, all I wanted was for him to fill me with his cum. A primal urge I couldn't explain even if I tried.

Jeremiah let out a guttural growl and buried his cock deep in my pussy. His jaw clenched tightly. His face twisted into a look that one only gets in the throes of orgasm.

"Yes, yes, yes," I screamed, cumming because he was. Knowing that I could do this for him was so hot, and knowing that he was filling me with his seed, even more so.

We came together, and it was the most intense orgasm I'd ever had.

From the way Jeremiah collapsed on top of me, barely holding himself up and breathing like he'd run a marathon, I had to imagine it was pretty intense for him too.

"Jesus," he said after a moment, lifting his head to look me in the eye. He kissed the tip of my nose before sliding out of me and rolling over to lay beside me.

He pulled me close, wrapping his arms firmly around my body. My head pressed against his chest, and his heart thundered loudly in my ear.

I had so many questions. Not just about Lauren and the case, but about Jeremiah's change of heart toward me.

So many questions, but I wasn't sure if I wanted to know the answers. I didn't want to ruin the moment. So instead, I rested against him in silence, listening to his breathing until it slowed and became rhythmic.

Eventually, I joined him in sleep.

OooOOOooo

I awoke to the sun streaming in the windows, and to an empty bed, and it wasn't mine.

I was in Jeremiah's bed, in his house.

I'd never seen his bedroom before and hadn't really looked at it the night before. I ran a hand over the down comforter wrapped around me. I fell asleep uncovered, but somehow ended wrapped up, safe and warm. A smile formed on my face as I pictured Jeremiah making sure I was taken care of before he headed into the other room to care for the twins.

Everything about his room was comfortable. Probably because everything in his room felt like Jeremiah. The head-board was carved from wood, likely by his own hand. There was a dresser made from the same wood in the corner, with the same intricate details as the headboard. An ottoman was at the end of the bed with his work boots sitting upon it. A desk against the window with photos caught my eye.

There was one with him and my dad fishing. I was only about eight at the time and standing with them, smiling with a tiny, pathetic fish at the end of my reel. I remembered that day; I'd been so proud of my fish. Jeremiah had helped me clean it, but I quickly learned I didn't have the stomach for that sort of thing. We ate my fish that night, and it sealed it for me - I didn't have the heart or the stomach for it.

But I remembered how Jeremiah had been so patient, even though my fish was nothing compared to the ones he and my father had caught. He made such a big deal about it.

A smile crossed my lips as I thought back to those days. We were all so young, even Jeremiah. My father had been a young father, having me at the age of twenty. Which meant that in that photo, Jeremiah and my father were the same age as I was now.

I heard footsteps in the hallway and turned my attention to the doorway. Jeremiah entered, fully dressed for the day, minus his work boots.

I nibbled my lip, unsure how the morning would go. Would Jeremiah have regrets again? Would he kick me out?

But he smiled at me as he entered. "Well hello there, Sleeping Beauty."

I sat up in his bed and let out a yawn. "What time is it?"

"Just after ten."

"What?" I screeched, pulling the blankets off me. "Why didn't you wake me? I have to be at work—"

He chuckled. "It's Saturday, Elle."

There was some relief, but not much. I usually still went in to work on the weekends, but there was a less strict schedule. I could go in at noon if I wanted to. Though I usually didn't. I preferred getting in early so I still had some semblance of a Saturday left.

I leaned back against the bed and joined Jeremiah in the chuckling. I didn't bother to cover myself.

Jeremiah noticed that right away, his laughter stopping. His eyes were as hungry as they had been the night before, taking in my naked body in full daylight. I took care of myself, and I took great pride in my appearance, so yes, maybe I was intentionally showing it off.

I wanted to wash away any doubts he might have. I wanted to remind him that I was a grown woman, not the child in the photograph on his desk.

"Elle, we need to talk about—"

I held up a hand to stop him. "I know, but before you say it was a mistake, please listen to me." I waited, expecting him to stop me and continue telling me it was a mistake. I continued. "Jeremiah, it's clear that we have something. We can't resist each other, no matter how hard we try. And I know you try. Maybe it's time to admit there's chemistry here, and there's nothing wrong with that. I'm a grown woman, you're a grown man, and we have something special, clearly."

I took a breath and waited for him to argue with me. But he didn't say anything. He walked toward me and sat down on the bed. He opened his mouth to say something when the baby monitor on the end table next to the bed sounded the alarm in the guise of a baby's cries.

"Naptime is over," he said with a chuckle. He was grinning, not arguing with me. There was no defensiveness. Nothing like I expected.

He hadn't responded, but he also hadn't disagreed.

Which considering it was Jeremiah, that was a damned good sign.

"Need my help?" I asked.

"Nah, I've got it."

"Alright," I said with a nod. "I think I need to head into the office for a bit."

Jeremiah nodded and left the room. I proceeded to get dressed, thinking over the last part of our conversation. As I stepped out of the room and into the living room, Jeremiah had his hands full, but both girls were content and no longer crying.

I wanted to stay and spend the entire day with them, but I had to look over the articles for the next week's paper. I had work to do.

And I didn't want to push my luck with Jeremiah either.

JEREMIAH

"Brody Pearson was called in today," Sam announced, sitting across from me at my dining room table. "Is there anything he might tell the Feds that could be a problem for you?"

Brody Pearson was a young, spoiled, entitled brat. The son of a developer, he'd been born with a golden spoon in his mouth. Not even thirty yet and already worth millions, thanks to daddy giving him a job that he otherwise wouldn't have landed on his own because he was a doofus.

He had no work ethic. Hell, he had no ethics, period.

I shrugged. "Nope. Never dealt with the kid. Can't stand him. His father isn't much better, though."

"Did you meet with either of them?"

I sighed. "I met with them early on, when they first came to town. They asked to meet with me to discuss new development they had planned for Liberty. Once I heard their plans and realized that, like the other developers who caused problems in this town, they wanted the lithium in the ground - well, I told them they could take their pretentious asses right out of Liberty."

"You didn't take any bribes to work with them, maybe give them priority over development deals?"

"Hell no. I don't want that garbage ruining Liberty. Do you really think I'm like that?"

Sam shook his head. "I know, Jeremiah. I know you're not like that. I just have to ask the questions I'd ask any client."

One of the babies cried out, giving me a reason to step away. I knew Sam was telling the truth - he had to ask. He couldn't assume anything. But I hated having my ethics questioned, especially by someone I considered a friend.

I hated that anyone would think I would work with trash like that.

I left the dining room and walked into the nursery. Amelia was sleeping peacefully, in spite of her sister's cries. I picked up Grace and double-checked Amelia, just to be sure she was fine. Being a new parent was scary, especially when I had no idea what I was doing. She was still breathing, just sleeping deeply. Maybe she was learning to sleep through the noise. If so, that might make things easier for me.

I rocked Grace in my arms, talking to her in soft tones, when Sam's voice piped up from the doorway.

"Have you thought about who might care for the girls if you do see jail time?"

I cringed. "No, because I'm not going to see jail time."

As I spoke the words, I knew I needed a plan. Just in case. I had to take care of these girls, no matter what. I had to plan for the worst and hope for the best.

"Do you know—"

"Can we talk about this out there?" I pointed to the hallway.

Amelia was sleeping, Grace was slowly going back to sleep. But it wasn't just that. I couldn't bring myself to talk about this in front of my girls. They were still too young to fully understand what was happening, but I still couldn't do it.

Sam nodded and stepped out into the hallway.

Grace fell back to sleep in my arms, and as much as it pained me to put her down, I knew I had to finish my meeting with Sam.

I had to clear my name. Not just for me, but for them too.

I exited the room and closed the door behind me, meeting Sam back in the dining room.

"You seem distracted today. Is everything okay?"

Is everything okay? Is he fucking serious? Of course it's not okay, I thought. *I'm being accused of crimes I didn't commit. My good name is being trashed. I might see jail time and lose my girls.* And that didn't even touch on the fact that I was sleeping with my best friend's daughter. That was my own doing, my own fault - and I found that I felt less and less guilty about it as time passed. But it still weighed on me.

"Yeah, just a lot on my mind," I answered. "I think that's to be expected, considering the circumstances."

Sam didn't take a seat at the table, so neither did I.

I wasn't sure there was much more to discuss until we knew more about Brody's statement. His father had been brought in earlier in the week but hadn't said much. It would be nice if one of them managed to clear my name, but I wasn't holding my breath.

"Alright then," Sam said, picking up his suitcase. "If you need to talk, you know where to find me. And if you figure out who you'd like to appoint as a legal guardian for the twins, I can draft something up for you."

I nodded. "Thanks, Sam. I'll give it some thought."

There was only one person I could think about that I'd trust with my girls. Someone I knew who would love them the way I did. A lump formed in my throat as I thought about the possibility of leaving them, but it made me feel better to imagine Elle caring for them in my place.

I saw Sam out and returned to the nursery. Both girls were sleeping peacefully now. They were little angels with delicate, pale skin and downy soft hair. They were still so tiny, as most twins are born premature. They weren't born too early; we were lucky they didn't have to stay in the hospital too long. Just a few extra days while Grace put some weight on. She was smaller than her sister, but only by a few ounces now.

They grew so fast. And even if I went to jail for only a few months, I'd miss so much. I couldn't bear to think about it, but I knew I had to make the call.

I stepped out of the nursery and stared at my phone, preparing to dial Elle's number.

Was I really doing this? Not just asking Elle to care for my girls, but everything else I was doing with her. After she left that morning, I thought about it long and hard.

She was right. We did have something.

I couldn't resist her; she was everything I wanted in a woman. But she was supposed to be off-limits.

Didn't mean I could resist her, though. Seeing her all worked up, so passionate to clear my name and do the right thing, I couldn't stop myself from kissing her. She was wrong about Lauren being involved, but that didn't matter.

She was doing it all for me. Well, for me and my girls. Which is why I knew this was the right thing to do.

I dialed the number and pressed the phone to my ear.

She answered on the first ring. "Jeremiah? Is everything okay?"

"Yeah, everything is fine. But we need to talk."

She was quiet for a second. "Okay... is this about last night?"

"Not really. It's about my girls. Listen, it's easier if we talk in person. Do you mind coming over?"

"Not at all. I'll be right there. I'm just leaving the office now."

"Perfect. Thank you, Elle."

We got off the phone, and I went into the living room to wait. I relaxed into the sofa, running a hand across my chin and beard. *What are you doing, Jeremiah? Carl would kill you.*

Would he though, I wondered? If I treated his daughter well, made sure she was happy and taken care of, would it really matter?

Of course I had no answer for that. Kind of hard to ask a dead man for permission to date his daughter.

Ooo000ooo

Elle was dressed down compared to her usual work attire. A pair of grey dress slacks, a light pink silk top similar to the one from a few days before, but with some lace detail at the collar and sleeves. The same pink and grey scarf was tied around her neck. A light grey wool coat completed the ensemble, along with matching grey hat and gloves since it was pretty cold outside.

"Brr," she said, stepping into the house. "The snow is really coming down."

"There's a fire going," I told her. "Come on. Let's get you in the living room.

I helped her out of her jacket, hanging it in the hall closet. She removed her gloves and hat, and even though she'd just been wearing a hat, her blonde hair still looked as flawless as ever. I'm not even sure how she did it, but she never looked not put together.

Except she had bedhead this morning, I remembered. And God, it was so sexy.

I didn't even scold myself for the thought. Instead, I smiled, and Elle smiled back at me, oblivious to the picture in my head of her naked, in my bed, her hair messed up from the sex we'd had the night before.

Elle took a seat in a chair close to the fire, I sat closer to the babies. I didn't get them too close to the fire in case it got too warm for them. Elle warmed her hands on the fire.

"So what did you want to talk about?" she asked.

Always straight to the point. I loved it. Most of the time.

"So I was talking to Sam earlier today, and he thinks I need to appoint a guardian for the girls. Just in case I do end up seeing some jail time."

Elle turned in her chair, no longer facing the fire. She stared at me with a dead serious look on her face. "You're not going to see jail time, are you?"

"Of course not," I said, brushing off the concern with a wave of my hand. Amelia dropped her pacifier and fussed, so I plopped it back in her mouth.

The two of them were in bouncy seats, and I'd been playing with them before Elle had arrived. But they felt the tension in me, like she'd told me, and had been fussy on and off all evening. I hated giving them pacifiers, but the little things seemed to calm them. And I wanted to do anything I could to make sure they felt calm and safe.

"So why are you bringing this up?" Elle's eyes narrowed in on me.

"Just in case, you know. It's probably a good idea anyway, just in case something happened to me or—"

"Nothing is going to happen to you." Her voice cracked.

"Elle, we never know what the future holds."

"I know, but you can't— I mean, you're not allowed to—" she stammered. I could see the tears welling in her eyes, imagining the worst.

I rushed to her side, wrapping my arms around her. She'd already lost so much. Her father had died unexpectedly, and he had been so young. It wasn't right, but those things happened.

And it could happen to me. A lot could happen to me, making it hard to raise my girls.

Elle rested her head against my chest, relaxing into me.

"I just need to make sure my girls are in good hands. Just in case, Elle."

She nodded, lifting her head. I wiped the tears from her cheek and stared into those deep, brown eyes. "Where do I come in with all this?"

"Well, if you'd be comfortable with it, I'd like to appoint you their legal guardian. You're the only person I—"

"Yes, of course," Elle interrupted, sitting upright to meet my gaze. "Of course, Jeremiah. You know I would do anything for those sweet babies. And you, of course."

"That's exactly why I'm asking you. I only trust you."

I took her hand in mind and gave it a firm squeeze. She turned her attention to the girls. "Here's hoping it doesn't come to that, but you can count on me to take care of them. No matter what."

"I know you will."

She turned her face toward me again, and I lowered my mouth to hers, kissing those sweet lips. She kissed me back, and it felt perfect. The warmth of the fire against my back, the warmth of her body to my front, and my girls safe and sound beside us. Everything just felt right.

It was hard to imagine anything could go wrong.

"The roads must be getting pretty bad out there," I stated.

"They are," Elle agreed. "And I haven't seen any salt trucks yet."

I nodded, smiling sheepishly. "Well, there's no way I'm going to let you drive in that weather."

"Are you asking me to stay the night?" A small smiled pulled at her lips.

"I'm not asking, I'm telling you. You're not leaving tonight, not with weather like that. I need to keep my girls safe. And that means all my girls."

She hugged me, standing up to wrap herself around me. Her lips pressed against my cheek, then moved to my mouth.

"I need to feed the girls and get them ready for bed," I told her.

"I can help. Then we can finish what we've started."

I didn't argue with her. What was the point? We both knew where this was headed, and I decided it was better to not fight it. Not where Elle was concerned. She would get what she wanted.

And I wanted it too.

ELLE

Jeremiah and I made a great team. I took one baby, he took the other. We fed them, bathed them, diapered them and had them in bed, passed out and happy, in record time. To think that he trusted me with his daughters meant a lot to me. To think that if the worst-case scenario became reality, I might be raising these girls alone.

I still lived with my mother. Not because I had to, but because I hadn't bought a place of my own yet. It hadn't been a priority. All my money, mostly inheritance from my father, went into the paper. The rest was tied up in some invest-ments. I wasn't rich, by any means, but I'd been able to stay on my feet and support the paper through some rough months.

But now I had to think about supporting two little girls.

As if Jeremiah could read my mind.

"You know I'm well-off. If something happens and you become their guardian, I would love it if you raised them in this house, and you would be taken care of. All three of you."

His construction business, prior to him taking over his father's position as mayor, had been highly successful. I didn't know how well off he'd been, but I knew he didn't have to struggle. He didn't even take a salary as mayor because he didn't have to.

His house was nice too. One of the nicer ones in the area, barring the ridiculous Holt mansion. He built most of the houses over by Violet's and James' homes; the entire neighborhood and development had been his doing. And it was exactly what the town needed - nice, comfortable housing that didn't hurt the environment and that fit right in with Liberty's current infrastructure. He was the type of developer we needed more of.

"We'll figure it out when the time comes, but hopefully it doesn't come to that."

He nodded, staring down at Grace, stroking her cheek. "Yes, but in case it does, you don't have to worry about anything. There's enough money in the bank to take care of all three of you, to pay for both of them to go to college, everything."

Like I said, I knew he'd been well-off, but that surprised me. He had more money than he'd let on. He never flashed around his money. No fancy cars or mansions. Instead, he'd put it away for his children's future.

Even though I thought I'd known Jeremiah inside and out, some things still surprised me. And it made me fall for him even more.

He walked over and put an arm over my shoulder, staring down at Amelia this time.

"They're so precious," I whispered.

"They are. I'd do anything for them."

"I know you would. You're an amazing father."

"You think so? Sometimes I feel like such a screw up."

"Jeremiah, seriously?" I stared at him to make sure he wasn't pulling my chain. How could he think that about himself?

He shrugged. "They're already in daycare, though not much, thankfully, and—"

"A lot of parents work and have to use daycare," I reminded him. "It's a fact of life, Jeremiah."

"It's not how I wanted to raise my girls, though. And had I not taken the mayoral position, I could have retired and—"

"Do you think you'd be happy in retirement?" I cocked an eyebrow. "Because I know you, and I think you'd get bored pretty easily."

"Maybe." He smirked. "But I could always act as an independent contractor, work on my own terms."

That was a good point, and more Jeremiah. He was a business-owner, someone who liked to work on his own terms, make his own schedule. He worked hard but preferred to work hard for himself.

But being mayor was different. He wasn't working for a corporation or CEO; he was working for the town. A town he loved.

I twisted around so I was facing him, and he wrapped his arms around my waist, holding me close.

"You are the most amazing father, Jeremiah. Not just that, you're the most amazing man I've ever met."

He raised his eyebrows. "Nah, that honor goes to your dad, Elle."

"Maybe. But you give him a good run for the money," I stated matter-of-factly.

Jeremiah's lips pressed against mine, and it wasn't the need-filled kiss from before, but one with something more behind it. Gentle and sweet. Just like the man he was on the inside.

"Come on," he whispered against my mouth. "Let's go to bed."

It wasn't even nine in the evening, way too early for sleep. But I wasn't about to protest.

Besides, I had a feeling we wouldn't be doing much sleeping.

Ooo000ooo

"One second," Jeremiah said, chuckling as he pulled away from my kiss.

I cocked my head to the side but let him go. He walked over to the desk, turning the fishing photo face down. I giggled to myself, not blaming him for not wanting to see a photo of me as a child with my father while we made love.

He came back to me, wrapping those thick, strong arms around me and lifting me off the ground. I squealed as he carried me over to the bed, depositing me against the warm, down comforter as gently as possible.

"God, you're so beautiful. I could just stare at you all the time."

"Please do more than just look at me." I giggled, holding my arms up.

Jeremiah smiled down at me, and that hungry look in his eyes returned. He fell onto the bed next to me, rolling us over so I was on top of him. We were both still fully clothed, to my dismay, but that didn't last long.

I ripped at Jeremiah's shirt, pulling the buttons free and likely breaking a few. He didn't seem to mind. He yanked my shirt off over my head and made quick work of my bra too. My breasts fell free into his hands, just enough for a handful. His rough fingertips brushed against my nipples and caused me to moan and grind against him.

He took one of them into his mouth, his tongue circling it as I rode his body, cursing our pants for keeping us apart.

Jeremiah flipped us around, sitting on his knees and pulling at my pants, sliding both them and my panties off at once. He removed his belt and pants, sliding them down and kicking them off onto the floor.

With both of us naked, he rolled us over again. I was on top, and my breasts were in his hands. His mouth explored my chest and neck, nibbling gently on my flesh. I rocked back and forth on my knees, rubbing against him. The feeling of his hardness against my clit teased me until I was dripping wet.

Every movement teased my opening and made me crave him more. Finally, when I couldn't take it anymore, I gripped him in my hand and guided him inside. Lowering my body, I gasped as he filled me. I was in control of how deep he went, but I needed all of him. I slid all the way down, as if my body was made for his.

Jeremiah gripped my hips, and I fell forward. His mouth found my nipple again as I bounced on top of him. It was like a nerve went straight from my nipple to my clit, sending sensations down below that were unbelievable and brought me to the edge immediately.

I came once, rocking back and forth on top of him, my clit rubbing against his pelvis and my nipple in his mouth. Jeremiah kept me moving on top of him as my body writhed and flailed from the pleasure.

As my orgasm subsided, I continued riding him. I moved up and down, grinding and rocking. I felt him against every inch of my insides, and I loved it.

Jeremiah released my nipple and cupped my face in his hands, bringing me closer to him. I fell forward and we kissed, deeply and passionately. His tongue moved in and out of my mouth much like his cock was moving in and out of my pussy.

My hands were on his chest, my nails digging into his

flesh as another orgasm hit me hard. My thighs cramped up, but Jeremiah helped keep me moving, prolonging the pleasure for as long as possible.

Then he held me close, rolling us over together, his cock never leaving my pussy. He hovered on top of me, plowing in and out of me, kissing me and touching me in ways I never thought he'd touch me. His rough hands moved over my body, exploring and savoring it beneath him.

I knew he was close.

Remembering how it felt when he came inside me, I was brought to the edge again. Thinking about him filling me with his seed, and maybe one day putting a baby inside me, brought to climax. I tightened around him as he throbbed inside me. We came together, our bodies rocking and writhing with pleasure until every last drop of his cum was spent.

Jeremiah lowered his head, resting his forehead against mine. He took a deep breath and opened his eyes, staring deep into mine. He kissed my lips and remained sheathed inside me.

We stayed like that for a few moments, kissing and touching, our bodies joined together.

If there was any regret left inside him, I didn't see it.

Ooo000ooo

I awoke the next morning, fully planning on staying in bed as long as possible. It was Sunday, and even though I spent many Sundays at the office, I'd planned to spend this one with Jeremiah and the babies.

I woke with Jeremiah that morning. He hopped out of

bed, ready to prepare breakfast for the girls. I threw on some clothes, ready to help him. I grabbed my phone out of my pants pocket, making sure it hadn't been damaged in last night's activities.

There was a missed call and a voicemail. I recognized the number right away.

Jeremiah saw the look on my face. "Everything okay?"

"Yeah, just a work thing. I'll check it later." I moved put the phone away, but Jeremiah must have read my expression, seen how badly I needed to take the call.

"I've got this," he said. "I'm used to making their bottles in the morning by myself. It's all good. Take the call, Elle."

"You sure?"

"I am."

He popped over to my side of the bed and gave me a kiss before leaving the room. My lips were still tingling with the warmth of his when I called Lauren Holt back.

"You wanted to speak with me?" she said dryly.

"Do you mind meeting me at my office later this afternoon?"

"I'd rather do it now," she said. "I have a family gathering later today."

I was surprised by how willing she was to meet with me, and I didn't want to press my luck. I hated leaving Jeremiah, but he was used to this. And besides, this was for him. I wanted to clear his name, and I thought maybe Lauren could help with that. Maybe she'd be willing to talk to me. After I witnessed what had happened at her parents', I thought perhaps she'd be more talkative than when the police had questioned her.

"Yeah, sure, give me about fifteen minutes or so to get into the office."

"I'll be there." She hung up the phone without saying goodbye.

God, I hated her. But I needed her. I had questions for her. I didn't want to upset Jeremiah by telling him the plan, so I told him it was a work thing. Not a complete lie.

Jeremiah kissed me goodbye at the door, a baby in each arm. I had to laugh at the sight, something I never thought I'd see, but he looked so natural.

And I was happy that I could be part of his little family.

I rushed into town, the roads having been cleared. Lauren was standing outside the office building when I got there. She was leaning against the wall, staring at her phone and tapping her fingers against her jacket impatiently.

"Finally," she muttered.

"I got here as quickly as possible," I said, unlocking the office door.

She hustled in as soon as the door was open, not so much as a thank you for holding the door open for her.

We walked into my office, and I shut the door even though no one else was there. Just a habit, especially since we were going to be discussing something very personal.

I took a seat at my desk and Lauren sat across from me.

"So I'm assuming this is about the interview the other day, and I can explain. I—"

I held my hands up. "It's not about that, actually."

She snapped her mouth shut in surprise and stared at me.

"I have a few questions about James Fitzhenry."

Lauren reached for her purse and began to stand up. "I already told the police and the Feds that I don't know anything."

"But your car was outside his place that night."

She stopped, putting her bag back down in her lap. She returned to a seated position. "What? That's not possible."

"So you weren't outside James' house the night he disappeared?"

"No, I—I was out of the country, as I told the Feds."

DADDY'S BEST FRIEND | 113

"For how long?"

"For almost a year."

"And you never came back to Liberty? Not at all during that time?"

"I don't have to answer these questions," she sniffed. "You're not a cop."

"No," I said, leaning back in my chair and steeping my fingers, carefully studying her. "Yet you're still here. You didn't storm out after I mentioned your car. Why's that?"

"Because I want to know what happened to James as much as everyone else. He was my ex, yes, but I still cared about him." Lauren kicked her chin out and stared me straight in the eyes.

"You know what I think? You killed him because he wouldn't take you back."

Lauren scoffed out a laugh. "Impossible. I wasn't even in the country, as I've said several times."

"If that's true, then why was your car outside of his place the night he disappeared?"

"I didn't even have my car at the time. My brother did because his was in the shop..." As soon as the words left her mouth, she realized they had been a mistake. She clamped her jaw shut and refused to look at me.

"So Alex was at James' place? Why's that?"

"There's no reason he should have been, and I don't believe that my car was outside his house." Her voice was weaker, less certain. She was hiding something, protecting her brother, but why? And from what?

"We need to tell the police about this."

"I'm done here," Lauren announced. She grabbed her purse, stood up, and hurried out of my office. I followed her, but she refused to say another word.

I followed her all the way to her stupid car, which looked so out of place on the streets of Liberty. It would look out of place anywhere, which is exactly why Violet remembered it. And I believed her.

Lauren got behind the wheel of her car and drove off. If she wouldn't go to the police, it left me with very little choice. Luckily, the sheriff, Teddy, and I were old friends. I had his number stored in my phone. I trusted him more than the Feds, so I called him while standing out on the street.

"Teddy, I think I have a break in the James Fitzhenry case."

I told him everything I knew.

JEREMIAH

Amelia and Grace were on the floor for some belly time, as Piper called it. Amelia was the stronger of the two, her head lifting off the ground easily. Grace was still getting there, but she was working her hardest.

I was on the floor with them, feeling a bit antsy. It had been a very long time since I'd spent this much time at home, not working. Even as a kid I was usually outside getting into trouble.

I had an urge to work, but not at the mayor's office. I wanted to build something. I'd made the girls' beds and nursery furniture, but that was the last time I'd touched a project. As a single father, I didn't have much time to do anything but care for Amelia and Grace.

But no matter how antsy I got, I really wasn't missing City Hall.

A knock came at my door, followed by Elle's voice. "Jeremiah, it's me."

I wasn't expecting her back so early. I got up and walked over to the door, keeping an eye on the girls as I did so. I opened the door, and as usual, Elle rushed into the house without so much as a greeting.

"There's a break in the case! I found something."

"Oh yeah?" I scratched my beard. "Was this the work thing from this morning?"

"Yes. I met with Lauren and—"

"Wait, you met with Lauren Holt? Why? This has nothing to do with the Holt family."

Elle smirked and shook her head at me. "That's what you think. So while Lauren wasn't in town, her brother had her car for a few days during the time of James' disappearance. Something about his car being in the shop or something."

"Stop, Elle. We don't even know if Violet's testimony is correct. She's not exactly a reliable witness."

"I know, I know," she said with a sigh, walking over to the girls and sitting down beside them with a smile. But her eyes were on me. "You should have seen her response when I asked about it, though. She knows something. I alerted Teddy to everything and—"

"What? You got the Holts pulled into this now too?"

I clenched my fists at my side and paced across the room. My head was spinning. This was a mess, and the more Elle helped, the messier it would get. Dragging Lauren into this wouldn't be good for anyone. I had to make her stop.

"Oh come on, Jeremiah. It's not like they're saints or anything. Even if they're innocent, I don't feel bad about having them investigated. I'm sure the police can find something in their shady ass background."

"Elle, please, I'm not going to ask you again. Let this go."

I couldn't even look at her at first. I feared my anger would show on my face, and I never wanted her to see me like that. But she needed to listen to me.

"I told you I'm not going to let this go. I'm doing this for you and the girls. And because you need to get re-elected, Jeremiah. Don't you want that?"

I turned on my heels. I was so fucking tired of that question. "What if I don't want to get re-elected?"

Elle's eyes widened, and she seemed genuinely stunned by my answer. She hopped to her feet. "Wait a minute. You're telling me you don't want to be mayor?"

"Are you surprised? I hate the public eye. I'm only doing this out of a sense of obligation."

"And because the alternative - George Holt - would destroy Liberty."

"I know," I admitted, my voice softening. I closed my eyes. "It's the only reason I haven't stepped down. I know all this. Doesn't mean I want it."

"Well you have to do this, Jeremiah."

My eyes popped back open. "If taking care of Liberty matters so much to you, why don't you run for mayor yourself?"

She gasped, at first acting like it was an insult. Then I watched as a realization fell over her face - maybe I'd meant it. Maybe I wasn't being sarcastic. A lot of emotions crossed her face and in her eyes.

I had initially spat it out in frustration, tired of being pressured. I'd been told for so long that there was no one else - and I'd believed it. But there was an alternative, and she was standing right in front of me.

"You've got to be kidding," Elle snorted. "Me? Mayor?"

"Why not?"

"Because...well, because I'm a journalist."

"Who's whip smart and passionate about politics and this town. I can't think of anyone better."

"Liberty has never had a woman mayor."

"You could be the first," I said matter-of-factly.

Elle began to pace around the room. I sat down by the

girls, feeling calmer than I'd felt in a long while. Maybe there was a happy ending for all of us. As long as I didn't end up in jail.

"You're joking," she said again.

I picked Amelia up in my arms, and the little girl cooed at me. "Not at all. I want to teach my girls that women can do anything men can do. Why wouldn't I believe the same about you?"

"Because..." She didn't finish her thought.

"I know it's a shock, but think about it, Elle. But not too long. The deadline to register as a candidate is coming up. But as far as I'm aware, you meet all the requirements."

She turned and stared at me with a weird look on her face.

I continued. "You attend every city council meeting for the paper already, you know what's going on in the city government. You've made connections with local businesses; I guarantee they'd support you. You're well-loved around here, Elle. You've lived here most of your life, bar the time you went away to college and interned. You've always had a passion for politics. You're perfect." *And not just for the mayor's position*, I thought but didn't say aloud.

"I have to think about this," she stammered. "I'm passionate about politics and Liberty, yes, but I always pictured myself working from the side lines. I can't– I mean, I don't know if I can do this right now. We have to clear your name..."

"Those are excuses, Elle. I know you better than almost anyone, and I know when you're doubting yourself. Stop it.

"But the case, Jeremiah."

"I want you to lay off the case, Elle. I mean it."

"I can't," she said softly, shaking her head emphatically. "And it's not just because I want you re-elected. I want to clear your name."

"I want my name cleared too, but you're getting too close to this. I'm worried about you."

Amelia cooed and gurgled, causing Elle's eyes to fall on the little girl instead of on me. The look on her face was so soft and full of love. She cared about my girls so much already. She cared about everyone. She had such a big heart.

I had to get her to listen to reason.

"I have to go. I have a lot to think about right now."

I didn't stop her. I still had Amelia in my arms and couldn't get up fast enough. She exited my house as quickly as she'd entered.

I sighed, worried that maybe she was getting too close to this.

No, no maybe. Clearly she was.

And I needed to convince her to back off. Not just for her well-being, but all of ours.

Ooo000ooo

I fell into bed late that night. Even though I wasn't getting much sleep lately, I knew that I'd probably have trouble falling asleep. No matter how tired I was, I couldn't shut my brain off.

Elle hadn't returned my texts or calls, which wasn't like her. I hadn't heard from her since I'd told her to back off. I couldn't help but worry about her.

I glanced over and saw the photo on my desk, still flipped over, but I knew the image by heart. I closed my eyes and remembered that day very well.

It was the day I'd decided I wanted kids of my own one day. Girls or boys, it didn't matter. Elle hadn't taken to fishing, sure, but that didn't mean we had a bad time. She scrunched her nose up when we cleaned her little fish, and later felt bad about killing it. I saw the innocence and love in her eyes for all living things and I respected the hell out of it. So often, we get cynical and burnt out as adults. We forget about the beauty in nature, the beauty of life.

I'd worked hard my entire life. I'd burnt out. Even back then, I worked hard and hardly ever played. But spending time with Elle back then had revitalized my soul in ways I never knew possible. I'd hoped I could father children of my own after that day. And I really wanted a little girl, just like her, if possible.

And now I had two.

I only hoped I'd be able to raise them as well as Carl raised Elle.

I hoped I could be there for them.

I opened my eyes and let out a deep sigh. It was so hard to reconcile the woman I was sleeping with and the little girl that tagged along adoringly after her dad. It still didn't sit right with me if I thought too long and hard about it, but there was detachment in my head when she was around. It was like they were two totally different people.

"I'm sorry, Carl." I wasn't sure if I said the words out loud or only in my head. Did it matter? It wasn't like he could hear me anyway.

I was apologizing not just for sleeping with his daughter - but that was a start. I was apologizing for dragging her into my mess. Not that I did much dragging; she threw herself into the pit all by herself. And deep down, I knew Carl would understand that part. He knew his daughter was hard-headed.

But me sleeping with her? Well, that he might not ever forgive. Maybe I was wrong and he would be fine as long as she was happy and treated well. I'd never know the answer.

But I'd do my best to take care of her.

I laid there, with my eyes closed for what felt like an eternity. Eventually, I did fall asleep - but I wished I hadn't.

Elle was standing at the end of the aisle, dressed all in white. A fairy tale wedding for a real-life princess, because that's what she was. A cathedral length veil fell down her back and covered the entire aisle. She turned and looked at me, her brown eyes so full of life. My eyes fell to her stomach.

She was with child.

And I was the groom, walking toward her.

I stepped up on the altar, and I looked down at my feet.

Blood. So much blood.

Any happiness was short-lived, since when I looked back up to try and locate the source of the blood, Elle was gone.

Her dress was on the ground in a heap.

I rushed forward, thinking maybe she was in that heap of white dress and found a woman there.

But it wasn't Elle.

It was Lauren.

Her dead, unblinking eyes stared back at me. Blood dripped from her nose and mouth and the back of her head. So much blood. It covered the floor and stained the white dress red. Even though she was clearly dead, her lips moved, "You did this to me, Jeremiah. It's your fault."

"I killed her for you, Jeremiah," Elle's voice spoke from behind me. "To clear your name."

I turned toward Elle, and the sweet girl that I remembered - the one from earlier with her eyes so full of hope and her belly with child - stared back at me with dark eyes. She was no longer pregnant. I glanced back at Lauren on the ground, her belly swollen with child. I'd been mistaken; it hadn't been Elle all along. It had been Lauren.

She was holding a knife covered in blood, wearing the same dress as earlier. The same one Lauren had been in.

"Elle, no," I stammered. "You don't understand. It's all a mistake. Lauren didn't do anything."

"She's a bad person," Elle said, walking toward me.

"This isn't you."

"I'd do anything for you, Jeremiah. Anything."

Her hands reached out for me, pulling me from the floor. When her lips touched me, I felt nothing.

I awoke with a start, sitting up in bed with sweat dripping down my brow. It was only four a.m. Still another couple hours, at least, before the girls would wake up for breakfast.

Elle would never do anything like that, I told myself. And I knew she would never kill anyone, not even Lauren. But knowing that she would do anything for me, well, that idea frightened me.

I climbed from my bed, knowing I wouldn't be able to sleep anymore. I would get started on a project, something to keep my hands busy. My mind too.

I knew that it was a nightmare, I knew Elle wasn't capable of anything like it, but she was getting too close to this situation, and I had to stop her before she did something she couldn't take back.

ELLE

"I can't believe I'm considering it," I said, nibbling on a piece of lettuce from my salad. I'd mostly pushed my lunch around on my plate, only taking a bite here and there to pretend I was eating. I didn't have much of an appetite.

"I can," Josie said, smiling at me across the table. "And I agree with him, you're perfect."

"I'm not perfect." I rolled my eyes. "Far from it, actually. I have no experience in politics."

"You've attended every single city council meeting."

"For the paper, yeah."

"But you know what's happening in Liberty. Probably more than anyone else."

"It gives me authority to write on it, but to actually run the city government? That's an entirely different set of skills."

"Which you have," Josie pointed out, taking a bite of grilled chicken.

"I don't have experience running anything like that."

"You've run the paper for a while now."

"The paper is different, Josie. It's totally different."

"Sure, but you're a smart woman, Elle. You know how

things work in the government, and I think you'd figure out anything you don't already know fairly easily. Everyone has to start somewhere. Do you think Jeremiah knew anything about city government before taking over?"

"No, but…" I really didn't have anything to finish that thought with. There was no but. She was right. He'd had no experience and even less knowledge of the government than I did.

"Exactly." Josie shrugged and offered an all-knowing smirk.

"I don't know. I'd have to act fast. The deadline to register as a candidate is coming up, and I'd need to get so much support in order to make it possible. Plus, I'd be running against Jeremiah."

"It sounds like he doesn't really want it," Josie commented. "I bet he'd drop out and support your run instead."

I opened my mouth to argue, to tell her that Jeremiah would never drop out. That he'd never give up on Liberty. And he wouldn't give up on our town, no, but if he believed in me, I could see him backing me as a candidate.

Which was just too much damn pressure. I rubbed my temples.

"What is it?" Josie asked. "More nagging self-doubt?"

"Always," I muttered, dropping my hands. "It just seems too complicated. What would I do about the paper? I couldn't do both at the same time."

Josie shrugged and gave me a look that said I wasn't going to like what she was about to say. "Maybe it's time to let the paper go. No one really reads print journalism anymore."

"I can't do that. Liberty needs their local news. The larger sources don't cover our small-town news."

"Right, but there are better ways to handle this. Perhaps an online paper?"

"I couldn't run it if I'm mayor."

"No, but I'm sure someone else could. Someone else in your office."

I bit into a cherry tomato, the explosion in my mouth a perfect metaphor for my life right now.

"Come on, Elle. We both know how passionate you are about politics and this town, and even though you don't say it, you're looking for something more than writing about high school basketball games and the occasional small-town scandal. You're smart, you deserve to do great things - and I think Liberty needs someone like you."

"You're my best friend, you're supposed to say those things," I muttered.

Josie laughed. "You're so difficult, you know that? I bet I could get everyone in this diner to vote for you. I bet Felicity would vote for you, wouldn't you, Felicity?" She called out to the woman behind the counter, another one of our friends. She owned the local diner and was someone I respected very much.

Felicity looked confused as ever, having not listening to our conversation. "Excuse me? Vote for what?"

"For Elle if she ran for mayor."

"Shh," I hushed Josie. "Don't talk so loud, I don't want the whole diner to know."

"Why? You afraid they might want to vote for you or something?"

Felicity walked over to our table and sat down across from me beside Josie. "You're running for mayor? That's awesome, Elle. And hell yeah, I'd vote for you."

My cheeks burned bright red, and I couldn't meet her eyes. "I don't know yet. I wasn't really planning on it, but Jeremiah suggested it." I kept my voice low, not wanting anyone to hear me talking about this seriously. The last thing I needed was for the local rumor mill to pick it up.

The front door of the diner rang, and Felicity's eyes moved in that direction. A small smile pulled at her lips as she slipped from the booth. "Excuse me, ladies. I need to help this next guest."

Felicity was the owner and had hostesses to greet the guests. I wondered who the VIP might be. Both Josie and I were curious and looked up at the same time.

Dr. Abel Hammond, Abe as he was called by the locals, walked in. He was an older man, around Jeremiah's age, and he and Felicity were deep in conversation.

"I wonder what that's about," I whispered.

"Maybe she's working your campaign already."

"Oh please," I said and rolled my eyes, turning back to Josie. "You have a one-track mind sometimes."

"Sounds familiar," she said and winked at me.

The door to the restaurant pinged again, but I didn't bother to look up. I was too focused on my salad, pushing the lettuce and tomatoes around on the plate. I wasn't hungry, though I knew I should be. My stomach was tied in knots.

"Eleanor Schaeffer," a male voice called out.

My head popped up so fast, I could have given myself whiplash. That voice sounded familiar. The tone wasn't friendly in the slightest either.

"Shit," I muttered.

Alex Holt was walking right toward me, his silky, sandy blonde hair brushed back, his designer glasses covering his eyes. He looked like he'd walked right out of a California photo shoot for the rich and spoiled.

"What does that asshole want?"

I had an idea.

I stood as he approached our table, wanting to shield Josie from the man as much as possible. But she stood up, standing beside me with her arms crossed in front of her.

Alex ignored her, instead pointing a finger in my face.

"You need to stay out of this. You know nothing about what's going on."

I shrugged. "I only told Teddy that you were driving your sister's car. If you're innocent of any wrongdoing, what does it matter?"

"It doesn't," he spat.

I had to admit, seeing him so unhinged intrigued me. He was normally so put together, always smiling for the camera. Putting on the act of the golden boy, the perfect son. To know he was this angry over such innocent information made me think there was more going on here.

He continued complaining, though I wasn't paying attention to most of it until he said, "You only dragged me into it because you can't find any other way to clear that asshole's name."

"Wait a minute. Did you just call Jeremiah an asshole? If that's not the pot calling the kettle black, I don't know what is."

Alex scowled, lowering his sunglasses so I could see those creepy ass eyes of his. I shuddered but tried to hide it. I wasn't going to let him intimidate me.

"He's not going to win re-election. No matter what bullshit you try to pull, you're not taking my family down with him. My father will be mayor of Liberty."

"Oh yeah? You're so confident about that, but I bet no one here would vote for him."

Alex scoffed. "Like they'll have a choice once Jeremiah is behind bars."

"He won't be behind bars, but even if he is, your dad won't be the only candidate."

"Oh yeah?" Alex chuckled, wiping his face with his hand. "Why, are you running?"

"Maybe I am," I stated, speaking louder than intended.

Alex doubled over in laughter, "Sorry, it's just—wait, you're serious?"

More laughter. No one else in the diner was laughing, though. And I was beginning to suspect he had more than a few screws loose. I'd always thought he was a douche, but this was a new site for me. He never made such a scene in public. I must have hit a sore spot.

"I don't see anyone else laughing here, Alex. Maybe you should be more concerned than you are." I narrowed my gaze and put my hands on my hips. Nobody laughed at me. Especially not a Holt.

Alex stopped laughing and wiped at his eyes. He still looked amused, but I knew his type well. He was trying to intimidate me. If he thought I was afraid of a little embarrassment, he didn't know me. Truth be told, there was nothing they could do to embarrass or shame me. My history was as clear as the sky on a summer's day in the mountains.

He had nothing on me. And I knew he knew it. That's why it scared him.

He steadied himself, cleared his throat and said, "Well, whatever happens, if you decide to run for mayor or not, it would be in your best interest to stay out of my family's personal affairs, Eleanor."

"Is that a threat? Because if so, there's a whole restaurant who heard you."

"Oh no, it's not a threat," he said with a sneer. "It's a suggestion." He turned on his heels and marched out of the diner, letting the glass door slam on the way out.

All eyes were on me now.

Was this it, was this how I was going to announce my run for mayor?

"Does this mean you're doing it?" Josie asked, beaming at me with pride.

"Maybe."

"Maybe? That didn't sound like a maybe to me," Josie said, punching me playfully in the arm.

I wanted it. I wanted it so stinking bad. Not just because I wanted to get back at Alex Holt for laughing at me, but because his family was awful. Truly awful. And I couldn't even let them entertain the idea of them running my town. They'd destroy everything Liberty stood for.

That was the moment I decided to go for it. I just had to figure a lot of other things out first. It wouldn't be easy, but as my daddy always told me - nothing worth having ever was.

Another idea hit me at the same time - what was causing Alex to become so unhinged in public? Maybe my gut had been right; the Holts were behind James' murder. But maybe it was more than that.

Maybe they were behind all of it.

I grabbed my bag and dropped some money on the table, enough to pay for both of our meals plus a nice tip. "Can you take care of the check, please?"

"Sure, but where are you going?"

"To register for the race," I said, speaking low so only Josie would hear me.

I'd announce it to the world later, once I announced it to my friends and family first. And after I talked to Jeremiah too. He deserved to hear it from me.

The Holts wouldn't win, I'd make sure of it.

JEREMIAH

"That's great, Elle. I'm so happy for you." Relief washed over me as she announced her intention to run.

"You sure you're okay with it? I mean, I get that you'd like to step down sometimes, but are you absolutely sure that once all this drama is over with, you won't regret it?"

I had the phone tucked between my ear and shoulder and was juggling both Amelia and Grace in my arms, rocking the girls who'd only just stopped crying. They'd been fed, changed, and were simply fighting sleep. Elle's question sounded even more ridiculous considering the context, but I didn't laugh.

"Trust me, it has nothing to do with this stupid scandal. I'm just not cut out for public office. You're much better suited for this than me."

"I guess so. I just feel bad."

"You shouldn't." There was a knock at the door. "Hey, I have to go? I think Sam might be stopping by, and I've already got my hands full."

"Alright. Talk to you later"

I wanted to ask her to come over but decided against it.

I'd call her back later. Right now, I needed to get off the phone and deal with Sam.

I put the babies down in their pack and play and hung up the phone as the knocking continued.

"Sam, you're really early, hold on."

"FBI, open up."

I froze just above Amelia's crib.

FBI? A moment of panic was followed by a reminder from my brain to calm down. It could be anything, I reminded myself. Maybe they had more questions. Something in my gut told me it was more than that.

I didn't even remember walking over to the door, but I opened it. And the next few moments happened so fast, I felt like it couldn't be real.

"Jeremiah Jenkins." An agent held up his federal badge. "You're under arrest for extortion, bribery, money laundering, and murder."

"What? No," I argued. "I'm innocent."

The federal agent had handcuffs ready if I wasn't willing to go on my own accord. All I could think about were my girls in the other room.

"Please, I need someone to call Eleanor Schaeffer to take care of my girls," I said. "I'll go with you, no need to cuff me. Just make sure my girls are taken care of, that's all I ask."

Teddy stepped into the house, and I was relieved. Finally someone I could trust. "I'll call Elle," he promised, patting me on the back with an apologetic glance. "And I'll personally wait here until she arrives."

I nodded. "Thank you." It was the best I could hope for. I knew I couldn't fight it. I had to do what the agents wanted me to do.

Even if this was a mistake.

My heart broke. I didn't want to walk out of that house, I

wanted to wait for Elle. But I knew I had to go freely or they'd cuff me and tack on resisting arrest.

Not in front of the girls. Even if they wouldn't remember it, I'd never forgive myself.

I dragged my feet, but I walked out the door surrounded by both sheriff deputies and Feds. They read me my rights, but it was all a blur. I knew my rights well enough to know one thing.

"Call my lawyer. I won't speak without my lawyer present."

One of the other deputies nodded. "Sam will meet you at the station."

Dickinson, the agent who'd interviewed me earlier, scoffed. "Small towns. The corruption runs deep."

"What's that supposed to mean?" the deputy, a young man named Henry, asked. I knew Henry, had watched him grow up in town. He was a good kid who turned into a good man, but he did have a smart mouth on him. Always did. He didn't take shit from anyone.

"It means, everyone knows everyone. Can't trust the local law to not be involved in the shit," Dickinson said. "Which is why we're here."

Dickinson shoved me into the back of a police car and slammed the door. I couldn't hear what else was said between Henry and him, but it didn't really matter.

None of them were involved in this, none of them were protecting me.

I was innocent.

But I no longer felt hopeful about the truth setting me free.

Ooo000ooo

Agent Dickinson tossed a file down in front of me. Sam, of course, grabbed it and looked it over first. I stared straight ahead at the detective without saying a word.

"Can you explain that?"

"Explain what?" Sam asked. "It looks like the same financials you had before."

"It is, except we traced the source for some of those transactions. We discovered an offshore bank account belonging to the Pearson family, and as hard as they tried to keep it a secret, the truth finally came out. And it's the one shown sending large sums of money in and out of the city coffers."

Sam closed the file and sighed. "My client didn't handle the financials. James Fitzhenry was the treasurer. He controlled money that came in and out of that account."

"But your client oversaw the accounts, didn't he?"

"He did…" Sam hesitated, but then cleared his throat and continued. "My client trusted James Fitzhenry and didn't monitor them as well as he should have. Jeremiah took over the job as mayor from his father, with no prior experience, and he relied on help from other departments, trusting Fitzhenry and others to run their own departments with very little oversight."

Looking back, yes, I'd screwed up. But I had never asked to be mayor. I did the best I could, and Sam was right - I had trusted James. He seemed like a good, honest man. The people trusted him. So did I.

"Well then, why would Fitzhenry come forward and give Jeremiah up, saying he forced him to handle that cash flow without telling him where it went or where it came from? And why is he dead now? Oh, that's right, you should keep looking in the file. Autopsy came back."

Sam picked the file back up and flipped through the pages

in it. His face turned as white as a sheet. "I need to speak with my client alone."

"Have at it," Dickinson said, the sound of his chair on the concrete floor was like nails on a chalkboard, but I was so relieved that he was leaving, if only for a moment.

When the door shut behind him, Sam turned to me. "The body was James Fitzhenry," he said slowly.

My heart ached for the guy. He wasn't a bad guy or my father wouldn't have trusted him as much as he had. Whatever his role in the crimes, I was certain it wasn't uncoerced.

Sam continued. "And it wasn't suicide. He was shot in the back of the head before his car was driven into the lake."

"Shit."

"You're a hunter, right, Jeremiah?"

"I am, but I haven't been hunting in years. What's that got to do with anything?"

"The gun used was a 270 Winchester."

"Yeah? It's a popular hunting rifle. Doesn't mean it was one of mine."

Sam nodded. "Do you have a lock on your gun cabinet?"

"I don't keep them in my home at all anymore. Because of the girls. I don't want to risk it with them in the house."

"Where do you keep them?"

"I have a storage locker where I keep my gun safe, but why does it matter?"

"I'm sure the Feds are searching that locker now. And every other piece of property you own."

"That's fine. They won't find a damned thing."

"Let's hope not," Sam said, not meeting my gaze. "Are you sure you're being honest with me, Jeremiah?"

"Of course I am," I said. "Why wouldn't I be?"

"Because they also found traces of your DNA in James' car and at his home."

My heart dropped. "I've never been to his house or in his car. Maybe it came off his coat or something."

Sam didn't look entirely convinced, but he reached out and patted my arm. "I'm sure there's a reasonable explanation, Jeremiah. If you insist you're innocent, I believe you."

"I *am* innocent," I said.

But I wasn't so sure that meant a damned thing anymore.

ELLE

I got to Jeremiah's as quickly as I could. Josie was with me, thankfully. I wasn't sure I could have driven on my own. After she paid our checks at the diner, she found me at City Hall just as I got the call. My heart was racing, and I couldn't believe this was happening.

Teddy left me in charge of the babies, who were screaming when I got there. Josie took Grace, I took Amelia.

"I'm thinking it's dinner time," I said, shaking all over.

"I'll prepare the bottles," Josie said. "Try to be calm."

Easier said than done considering the circumstances, and with two crying infants to care for. Josie had a son of her own, so she knew what she was doing. She placed Grace beside me in the pack and play and hurried to the kitchen.

I walked over to Grace, still cradling and rocking her sister in my arms.

"I promise you girls, I will clear your daddy's name. He's a good man and doesn't deserve any of this."

"Who are you talking to?" Josie called from the kitchen.

"The babies," I said. "Trying to calm all of us down."

"Keep talking then," Josie said. "Do whatever it takes."

Amelia had started quieting down a bit in my arms. I knew once they had their bottles, they'd be even happier. I'd nannied before, and I had experience babysitting, but never two at once. And never as their sole caretaker either. I was always there to assist the parents or to watch the kids for a few hours.

But I had no one else to take over for me once Josie left.

Now I knew how Jeremiah felt, and I understood his stress all too well.

That poor man.

Josie came back into the living room, two bottles in hand. She took Grace again, and we sat on the couch together in silence, feeding the babies.

"They were hungry, poor babies," Josie cooed. "They've been through so much."

"I know," I said, wiping the tears from my eyes. I felt very emotional about everything. "Neither of them deserve this."

"No, they don't," Josie said, rubbing my arm. "But they've got you. They're in good hands."

"I hope so," I said, looking down at the baby in my arms. I'd never felt so unsure of myself. Not even when it came to the whole mayor thing. This was a million times scarier.

Josie stayed with me and helped me put them to bed, but she had her own family to get home to. She couldn't stay too late, even if she wanted to help.

"I'll be fine," I said, faking a smile to hopefully reassure her. I didn't want to keep her too late.

"I'm just a call away, and if I can't come over, Leah or Piper or Felicity can. We're all here for you."

"Thanks, Josie," I said, giving my best friend a hug.

I held it together until she left, but once the door was closed, I slid down to the floor. The tears finally fell, and I let them. I was alone, the babies were asleep, and I could finally let loose.

My phone vibrated in my pocket, and I tried my best to wipe away the tears as if the person on the other end could see them. I cleared my throat and hoped I didn't sound like someone who'd just been crying.

I checked the caller ID. It was a call from the local jail.

I answered right away. "Jeremiah?"

"Yes, it's me. I've only got a few minutes, but I wanted to make sure everything was alright with the girls?"

"I'm here with them. Josie was here too. We took care of them. They're fed and asleep now."

He breathed a sigh of relief. "Thank you. Are you okay?"

"Shouldn't I be asking you that question?"

"Well, we both know how I'm doing."

"I know, and I'm sorry. I'm still trying to clear your name."

"No, Elle. Please, just don't get involved. You need to take care of yourself and my girls."

"I need to take care of the people I love too," I insisted, my voice strong. "You know that's who I am, Jeremiah."

"I don't have time to argue about this, Elle. But please, take care of yourself and the girls - no matter what happens. Please."

"Nothing bad is going to happen. It can't." Jeremiah was quiet. "I'm going to prove that the Holts are behind this. Lauren's car was outside his house, and either Lauren or Alex was there the night he disappeared."

"Elle, just take care of the girls and yourself. Stay at my house, it's your home now too. That's all I want from you. Let my lawyer handle the rest."

"Jeremiah, I—"

"Sorry, time's up. I have to go."

The line went dead as if cut off by someone other than

Jeremiah. I wasn't sure if they had strict time limits before the phones shut off or if Jeremiah had hung up on me. Either way, it left me feeling empty. I had no idea what to do with myself.

And I had to do something. God knew I wouldn't be able to sleep, and I couldn't just sit on the floor crying all night.

I picked myself up off the floor and walked through the house, from room to room, looking for things to do. I picked up the toys and blanket from the floor from when they had tummy time earlier and put those away. I cleaned up the kitchen, washed the bottles. I took out the trash. I was running out of things to do since Jeremiah kept his place pretty spotless.

I wandered into his bedroom and picked up the photo on his desk, putting it back in place. Jeremiah looked so young back then. He still had a young face, but nothing like when he was twenty-eight.

He had no idea where his life would take him back then.

Hell, neither did I, but I was only eight. I had so much life to live.

And so did Jeremiah. He still had so much life to live. And he had his daughters to live *for*.

I began straightening his desk, without even thinking. It just happened. I needed to keep moving, keep busy. I picked up a check book, laughing at how outdated Jeremiah was. I flipped through it absentmindedly, but there was only one check written.

For $100,000.

My curiosity got the best of me and I checked to see who it was written out to.

L. Dierks. I had no idea who that could be. Dated for April third. About ten months prior.

Only one check was written out of the entire check book. That was it.

I wondered, briefly, if that was for the mother of his children. I had no idea who she was. Some surrogate, I assumed. It would make sense that he paid such a large sum of money to her for that, but with everything else going on, I wasn't sure what to think anymore.

JEREMIAH

"You have a visitor," the guard said as he opened the door to my cell. I stood up from the cot they'd given me to sleep on and walked over to the door where he cuffed me.

I'd never been behind bars before, and God willing, I wouldn't be there for long. I did what I was told, letting the guard lead me down the hall to a room.

There was a table in the center of the room, and Elle was sitting there. When the door opened, she jumped up, and her eyes were so full of pain as she saw me in handcuffs and an orange jumpsuit. It pained me just as much to have her see me that way.

The guard walked me over to the table and let me sit down.

"You can take those things off," Elle said, chin up. "He won't hurt me."

I didn't think her words had any bearing on the guard removing the cuffs, but it was a nice gesture on her part all the same. She seemed angry that I was there. At least I wasn't the only one. She watched as the guard left the room, staying silent until the door was closed behind him.

142 | K.C. CROWNE

"Oh Jeremiah," she said, reaching across the table and taking my hands in hers. "I'm so sorry this happened."

"Where are the girls?"

"They're with Piper," she said. "They're in good hands."

I nodded, unable to look her in the eye. I was so ashamed, even if I hadn't done anything to deserve being in here.

"What's the plan?" she asked.

"The plan?"

"Yes. When do you get in front of a judge, when can you make bail, you know - the plan." She sounded so professional, so put together. Almost like a lawyer herself.

"I get to see a judge this afternoon."

"And what's the plan?" she pestered.

I sighed. I really didn't want to drag her into all of it, but I had to keep her in the loop. "I plead not guilty. Because I'm not guilty. Simple as that."

Sam had mentioned the possibility of a plea deal. If I pled guilty to the extortion charges, they would go lighter on the murder charges. I would face jail time - a lot of it since a man was dead. But there was no way in hell I'd plead guilty to something I didn't do, especially murder.

My babies wouldn't grow up thinking their daddy was a murderer or an extortionist. Especially since I'd still miss out on them growing up. It wasn't like I'd be released with just a slap on the wrist. I'd miss first steps, first birthdays, Christmases, their first days of school. I might be able to get out when they were fifteen years old, but by then, they wouldn't even know me.

It hurt to even think about missing everything.

Elle was studying my face and slipped her hands from mine. She put some distance between us.

"What is it?"

"What is what?" she asked, blinking at me in surprise.

"I can tell there's something on your mind. Spit it out."

She sighed and leaned back in the chair, twirling a section of her hair. Her hair was down today, falling over her shoulders with a hint of natural wave to it. She wasn't wearing makeup, and she looked as if she'd just gotten out of bed and put whatever she could find on. This wasn't like her, but she also never had to care for two babies alone before either.

"I found something, Jeremiah. And I don't know what to make of it."

I raised my brows. "What did you find?"

"A check," she said. "Written for a very large amount to an L. Dierks."

I put my face in my hands, letting out a deep breath. I had to explain it to her, couldn't get around that.

"I know it looks bad, but I swear, Elle. The check was written out to the mother of my girls. When we first found out she was pregnant, she was scared and not sure what to do. She was thinking of aborting the pregnancy, but we talked about it. I told her I'd raise the baby. We didn't know it was twins at the time. She needed help, so I supported her throughout the pregnancy, through wire transfers. But that night, I had my check book in the car and figured it would be faster than setting up a transfer. "

"So L. Dierks is the mother of your children?"

"Yes."

"She wasn't a surrogate then? It wasn't pre-arranged?"

"No, not at all. We had a one-night stand that resulted in pregnancy. She didn't want to be a mother. I told her I would take care of the baby and raise it; she wouldn't have to be part of its life. We made an arrangement, and since her situation is so dangerous, I promised to keep her identity a secret."

Elle nibbled her thumb nail, another habit I'd never noticed. This entire situation was doing a number on her, and I felt terrible for it.

She nodded, seemingly okay with the answer.

A guard opened the door and called out. "Time's up."

"My hearing is today at two," I told her. "Hopefully I can make bail and be home by dinner time."

Elle nodded, not saying another word. I was led from the room and put back in my cell. Thankfully, I was alone, I had no cellmate. But that meant I had nothing to do but stare at the walls and get caught up in my head.

And the thoughts in my head were likely as unfriendly as any cellmate might be.

Ooo000ooo

"How do you plead, Mr. Jenkins?" Judge Beverly Slade sounded bored as she spoke to me. She'd read the list of charges a moment before, and my head spun. There were so many of them, none of which I was guilty of. How did I find myself in this mess?

"Not guilty, Your Honor." Sam had brought up the deal again, but there was no way. None. I wasn't guilty. I was going to prove it.

There was a lot more legal speak, all of it sounding like something out of a television courtroom drama. I never expected to find myself in front of a judge.

"We request bail be denied for the defendant," the prosecutor spoke up.

"On what grounds?"

"He's a flight risk, Your Honor,"

I scoffed at the very thought.

"The defendant has two infant children and no known

family outside of Liberty. He does not appear to be at risk for leaving the area. Bail will be set at one million dollars."

One million dollars. My heart skipped a beat. Sam had told me it was possible they'd ask for a very large amount for my bail, even mentioning a million himself. Murder charges were serious, and it was possible I wouldn't have been given bail at all - except my record helped me. It was clean and clear, not so much as a parking ticket.

But I was going to be released.

I was going home to my babies.

Elle picked me up outside the jail some time later. She was alone; the girls were still with Piper. I swore to myself as soon as it all was over I'd be spending every minute with my girls. I'd never leave their sides again if I could help it.

She drove me straight to the daycare, and we picked them up. I didn't stick around for small talk, all I wanted was to get us home. All of us. Including Elle.

I didn't say much, and neither did Elle. I wasn't sure if she just didn't know what to say or if she was mad at me for not being more open about the mother of my children. It didn't matter, as far as I was concerned. She wasn't in the picture. I preferred not to think about her. The girls would never know her because that's what she wanted.

So in my mind, she didn't exist. I was thankful for her for giving me the girls and for giving me the option to raise them alone even though she had no desire to be a mother. Her situation was difficult. There was no ill will. But I tried not to think about her as much as possible. It was better for both of us if we forgot she existed.

"Jeremiah?"

"Yes, sorry," I said. "Did you say something?"

"We're home," Elle said. "I can grab Amelia, if you can get Grace."

"Of course." I shook myself out of my thoughts. It did me no good to live in the past.

We carried the girls inside, hurrying in since the snow had started to fall again. It was getting cold since the sun went down. They were covered up, but I wanted them inside, safe and warm.

Elle helped with the bottles while I got the fire going. We fed the girls in the warm glow of the fire, and it felt nice. I had never appreciated my home more than that moment, after a night spent behind bars.

Hopefully I'd never have to do it again.

"Grace lifted her head up yesterday, all on her own," Elle said softly.

"That's my girl," I cooed. "So proud of her."

"They're getting so big and strong," Elle mused, taking Grace's little hand, letting the fingers wrap around one of hers while she fed the baby.

"They are." And I could miss so much if I end up behind bars. I cleared my throat. "If I end up going to prison, I could be gone for a very long time."

"Don't talk like that."

"I have to because it could happen," I said. "And if that's the case, and you're still comfortable caring for them, I expect you may find someone else - another man - and—"

"Jeremiah, stop."

"No, Elle. You need to listen to me," I said, gripping the bottle tighter in my hand. Amelia finished it, and I put it down on the coffee table, slamming it down a little harder than necessary. "If I go to prison for twenty or more years, the girls won't even know me. And I can't expect you to wait for me."

"I will. I waited this long for you, didn't I? I waited for my entire life, and—"

"Most of that was your childhood, Elle. It doesn't count.

You're a grown woman with needs, and you deserve a happy family. So do the girls."

Grace finished her bottle, and Elle put it down. She lifted the baby up to rub on her back, since Grace sometimes got reflux. She knew all this, and she acted without direction. But her gaze never left mine.

"We don't know what's going to happen, but you can rest assured, I'll do everything possible to make sure you're the one raising your daughters."

"I appreciate that, but you need to stay out of it, Elle."

She pursed her lips, and I knew that look. She wasn't going to stay out of it, and there was nothing I could do to stop her.

God, she was a strong-willed woman.

And I loved her for it.

She was so beautiful, holding my child. Her blonde hair pulled to one side, away from Grace's prying fingers. Her brown eyes might have been tired, but she was alert. She was smiling in a natural sort of way. Contentedly. As if she this was exactly where she wanted to be.

And I knew in my heart, it's exactly where we were both supposed to be.

ELLE

Jeremiah pressed me up against the bedroom door. The girls were asleep, and we were finally alone. He'd been quiet all evening, so this sudden change in his behavior took me by surprise.

His lips melted against mine, his beard tickling my face. God, I loved this feeling. I loved everything about it.

He pulled his lips away, but our bodies were still touching. I could feel his erection through his jeans, pressing into my belly.

"Are you going to tell your mother about us?" he asked.

His question surprised me. "Um, I don't know. Should I?"

His forehead pressed into mine, his eyes even with mine. "I think so. Since it appears this is going somewhere, but…"

"But what?" My pulse raced. What was stopping him from making this official?

He reached up and pushed a strand of hair behind my ear. "But let's wait until after the trial. If I end up behind bars, then it doesn't matter anyway. We can't be together."

"You're not going to end up behind bars," I whispered. The tears stung my eyes. Normally, I was a realist. I would look at the facts and see that there was a chance he could end up in jail. But I couldn't think like that. It hurt too much.

All my life, I'd wanted this – I'd wanted a life with him. I had my chance, and now it could all be torn away.

He stroked my cheek, his hands rough against my skin. I closed my eyes and leaned into his touch. *Everything will be alright*, I told myself. I felt safe with him, like nothing bad could happen as long as Jeremiah was at my side.

"After the trial, we'll tell people about us," he said.

Us.

We were an us.

He kissed me again, moving me away from the door, and pushed it open. We stumbled inside, pulling at each other's clothes and giggling like teenagers, while also trying to remain quiet. Once naked, Jeremiah swept me into his arms and threw me onto the bed, falling along with me. We rolled around, kissing and touching and exploring each other's bodies like it was the very first time. I ended up on top of him.

He cupped my face in his hands, forcing me to look into his eyes. "I love you, Elle."

My heart skipped. "You—you do?"

"I do. I love you. You don't have to say it back. I'm not expecting you to right away, it's just—p"

I silenced him with a kiss, my hands pressing against his on the bed beneath me. "Of course I love you," I said with a giggle. "I've always loved you."

"Not like that, of course," he said.

"As soon as I realized what love-love was, yes, I did," I assured him. "Even while in New York City, I loved you from afar. It's always been you, Jeremiah. No other man has ever compared to you, and I feared I'd be single forever because no one ever would."

We kissed some more, his tongue pushing into my mouth

and stealing my breath away. His hands ran along the sides of my body, up and down, until he grabbed my hips, helping me rock back and forth on top of him - rubbing his cock between the lips of my pussy, teasing me.

He rolled us over, pressing his body against mine. His lips moved down to my neck, then my chest. He took one of my nipples between his lips, causing me to shudder.

Our bodies connected and found each other like old friends, and with one, solid thrust, he was sheathed inside me - where he belonged. Our bodies moved and rocked, and we were in our own little world. Nothing else existed in that moment, just us and the pleasure we shared between us.

Jeremiah leaned back on his thighs, staring down at me with hungry eyes. The way he looked at me always took my breath away, he made me feel beautiful and cared for. But now, I knew it was more than just caring about me.

He loved me.

I came once like that, staring at that marvelous man, feeling him moving in and out of my body with precision. No one made love the way he did. I was sure he had to be the best in the world. I came hard, grabbing onto the sheet as my body shook wildly.

Jeremiah continued pumping in and out of me until my orgasm subsided. He slipped out of me, then flipped us around so I was on top. He was sitting up, his back against the headboard, and I straddled his lap.

I slid down him, riding him and grinding against him, the headboard knocking against the wall from the momentum of our fucking.

Jeremiah moved me up and down on top of him, pulling my ass down hard onto his lap. His face twisted into that all-familiar look. I leaned in, pressed my lips against his, and said, "Cum inside me, Jeremiah. I'm close."

My thighs trembled as another orgasm hit me like a wave.

Jeremiah pulled me down, held me in place, filling me with his seed.

It wasn't until afterward that it hit me. I really needed to get back on birth control. If this were to become a regular thing, and it sounded like it would, I needed protection. It just hadn't been a priority before, and I'd been stupid not to have been more careful.

But it was too late now.

I stayed in his lap, and he held my face in his hands, kissing my lips, my cheeks, my neck anywhere his mouth could touch.

"I love you, Elle."

Hearing those words caused my heart to race. I wasn't sure I'd ever get used to hearing them.

"I love you too, Jeremiah. So very much."

Ooo000ooo

"Alright, well, if you need anything, I can come home at lunch and—"

"Go to work, Elle," Jeremiah said, a baby in each arm. "I'll be fine."

"Are you sure?"

"I've been alone for most of the last two months," he said with a smirk. "I think I got it."

I knew Jeremiah could handle it, but I wanted to stay with them. But work called; the paper wouldn't publish itself. I still had to finalize the proof and send it out for printing and needed to do it all that day if we wanted to the paper to run on time.

I kissed Jeremiah, then kissed the foreheads of the cutest babies in the world.

"Have a good day," I said to Jeremiah. "If you hear anything about the case or your trial, let me know, please?"

"Of course," Jeremiah said, grinning at me. "Now go. And don't forget to turn the paperwork in to City Hall."

On top of everything else, I was running for mayor. Jeremiah would step down and support me once everything was in order. I had to get that done while continuing to work and see what I could find out to help him. He'd asked me to step back from the case, and I had - a little. I wasn't going to give up entirely. I just didn't have any new leads, no new information. The Holts weren't going to speak to me. Lauren was avoiding my calls. She had realized her mistake and had shut her mouth. I knew I wouldn't get anything else from her.

I had to hope for a break, something or someone to come forward with some information.

The trial date was set; we had several weeks to go. They'd torn apart everything of Jeremiah's and had found nothing. Even his gun was in storage, where it was supposed to be, showing no signs of being used recently. But of course, he had a nice collection of shotguns, and they argued it was possible he had another that was no longer in his possession. Until they found the exact gun that was used in the murder, Jeremiah was still the prime suspect.

I headed out the door and hopped into my car. There was another concern on my mind. I dialed Josie's number and put her on Bluetooth as I drove.

"What's up? Pretty early for you to be calling," she said.

"Yeah, so, I know it's probably too early to be freaking out, but my period is late."

"It's way too early to take a test, Elle."

"I know, and it's still early enough that it will probably

come, but I needed to talk to someone about it. I can't believe I was so stupid."

"You're not on the pill?"

"Well…no, not anymore. I didn't see a point since I wasn't sleeping with anyone, and things just sort of happened with Jeremiah. It happened so fast that it didn't even hit me until last night. Like, how could I be so stupid?"

"Relax. First thing, let's get you on some birth control or use some condoms since there's a decent chance you're not pregnant still. How late are you?"

"Only a day," I said, nibbling my lip. "If even that."

"You've been later than that before, girl."

"But I was also not having unprotected sex at the time."

"Yeah, I get it. But it's too early to freak out. It's way too soon for you to know anything."

I was just being paranoid. I'd been stupid, but I could still fix this. My period would come, and I'd be careful from here on out. "Okay, yes, I knew you'd talk some sense into me. Thank you. It's just—Jeremiah has his hands full as it is. I can't imagine him having a third baby on top of it all."

"Yeah, but you're not pregnant. Keep thinking good thoughts, Elle."

What if those good thoughts included actually being pregnant? *No, it's not right,* I scolded myself. I wanted a baby of my own one day, but now would be the worst possible time for that. *One day, Elle. One day. Not now.*

I hung up with Josie as I drove into town. I pulled into the *Liberty Leader* parking lot, and I was the first car there as usual. I walked into the building, flipped on all the lights, and went into my office. The first thing I did was check with all my sources, see if there was any news that needed to be added into this week's paper before it went to print. I opened my email and scrolled through.

An email from a John Doe caught my eye. The subject read *You should see this.*

I clicked on it, and it led to a video clip. The video was grainy with no sound. It appeared to be a security camera in the back alley behind several businesses in downtown Liberty. I zoomed in to see who was in the video.

Brody Pearson, the son of the local developer caught in the scandal, was seen clearly. His smarmy face was hard to miss. He looked right at the camera a few times, albeit unknowingly.

It looked like a business transaction, but why in a back alley?

The person with Brody was hard to make out at first because he or she wasn't in the frame. But then a woman stepped into frame and took a suitcase from Brody.

"Elizabeth, you old bat," I gasped. "I didn't know you had it in you."

No one else appeared, just Elizabeth Holt and Brody making some sort of exchange in in secret, in the dark. I had never looked too much into Elizabeth. She had always registered as a non-entity to me, someone who happened to marry into the mess. I blamed George for everything, ignoring the wife behind the scenes. It hit me how sexist it was to assume Elizabeth was just an innocent bystander in George's crimes. I dismissed her because she was a woman and because she was just so good at acting the part of a ditzy housewife.

Well, she registered on my radar now.

The video ended when the two of them disappeared off the screen. I sent the video to Teddy immediately in case my anonymous source hadn't done so already. Then I went straight into my database, typing in Elizabeth Holt's name.

Her photo popped up, along with the usual information. Her date of birth. Her marriages. She had divorced before marrying George. Two kids, yes, I knew that. Maiden name was Elizabeth Ann Dierks.

Dierks.

Huh. That's not a common name, I thought.

I leaned back in my chair, feeling like the wind had been knocked out of me.

L. Dierks was the mother of Jeremiah's daughters. Or so he said.

What the hell?

JEREMIAH

"You're home early." Elle popped into the house without so much as a knock. I'd given her a key that morning. "I told you I had this under control—"

Elle's face ended my conversation. Something was wrong.

"Who is L. Dierks?" she asked, crossing her arms in front of her.

I tried my best to fight off the frustration. "I told you, she's Amelia and Grace's mother. I paid her because she needed financial support during the pregnancy."

Elle chewed on her cheek and glared at me.

I had a sleeping Amelia in my arms. Grace had already fallen asleep in the pack and play. I didn't want our conversation to wake them up, and from the way Elle was looking at me, it was about to get heated very fast.

"Let me put them in the nursery."

Elle didn't protest. "I'll be in the kitchen. We need to talk."

I put the girls to bed, shutting the door behind me. The kitchen was far enough away from the nursery, so hopefully any shouting wouldn't wake them.

When I found Elle in the kitchen, she had a beer and was sitting at the table.

"So tell me again, L. Dierks. She's the mother of the girls, but she was in a situation where she needed money, huh?"

I took a seat across from her. "Yes, I told you all that."

"So L. Dierks isn't Lauren Dierks Holt?"

My heart skipped a beat. "Why do you ask?"

"Because I found out today that Elizabeth Holt's maiden name is Dierks, and that's not a very common name. Now either this is a huge coincidence, you've somehow managed to find one of Elizabeth's long-lost relatives and gotten her pregnant, or the L stands for Lauren - or even worse, Lizzie, which is short for Elizabeth. Which is it, Jeremiah?"

I opened my mouth to answer her, but I really wasn't sure what to say. I had to protect the girls.

"Because the Holts aren't hurting for money, so even if it was Lauren, why would you need to pay her all that cash?"

"I can't answer that."

"Why not?"

"Because I can't, Elle." From the look on her face, that wasn't good enough. And I didn't blame her. "Do you still think I'm innocent?" I asked her. "Do you still trust me?"

"I think you're innocent, yes, but I hate to admit, this recent revelation is making me wonder. If you'd just talk to me, I'm sure there's a logical explanation, but unless I hear one - what else am I supposed to assume, Jeremiah?"

I flinched. "I can't talk about it, Elle. You're the press and—"

As soon as I said those words, I'd known they were a mistake. Her face was a mixture of fury and pain. I pushed up from the chair and walked across the room to the sink. I stared out the window, trying to focus on anything but what was happening now.

"You trust me with your girls, even allowing me to raise

them if you go to prison. But you can't trust me with this? You can't trust me to put you and the girls above my job?" Her voice was thick with disgust and hurt. And I couldn't blame her for that.

She didn't understand. The girls' lives were at stake here. If I told her and it somehow got out, it would be a disaster. But it was Elle. I could trust her.

I turned around, "Elle..."

But she was gone.

I heard the front door slam. I'd waited too long; she must have taken my silence for an answer.

Maybe it's for the best, I thought. Still, knowing that I'd hurt her, that she didn't believe I trusted her, killed me. I slammed my fists down on the counter, thankful the girls were across the house, safe in their rooms.

This is why I doubted being a father to them. Everything I touch turns to shit.

My phone vibrated in my pocket, and part of me hoped it was Elle. But I knew she wouldn't be calling me this soon.

"Hey, Sam. Please tell me you're calling with good news."

"On the contrary. There's been a break in the case, but it's not good for you, Jeremiah."

I gripped the counter and closed my eyes. Great. Could it get any worse? How could there be a break that tied me to crimes I didn't commit?

"Go on."

Sam sighed. "A video surfaced that showed Elizabeth Holt accepting money from Brody Pearson. They've managed to link the Holts to the case."

"That should be good news for me, so what am I missing?"

"The Feds linked the transfers in your account to Lauren Holt."

Dammit.

Sam continued. "And while the initial witness who saw Lauren's car in front of James' house was deemed unreliable, the Feds pulled up some security camera footage from the neighborhood that showed Lauren's car driving through the night before James disappeared. So now it looks like you may have paid the Holts to kill James Fitzhenry, though none of that makes sense either. They're still trying to piece it all together, but I'm afraid the final outcome won't look good for you."

"It wasn't Lauren. It couldn't be."

"I wouldn't worry so much about Lauren Holt, Jeremiah. You need to worry about saving your own ass at this point. You need to tell me everything so I can help you."

"I'll call you back."

"What?"

"I need to make a phone call, then I'll call you back."

Sam was quiet for a few moments, likely exasperated by me at this point. Not that I blamed him. I was getting pretty tired of all the secrets too.

I had info to share with him, info I didn't think would be relevant. But apparently it was. And it would hopefully not only save my ass, but someone else's too. But at what cost, I wondered?

"Fine," Sam said.

"It might be tomorrow, but I promise to tell you everything I can."

I hung up and dialed another number straight away.

"Lauren, we need to talk. Now."

OooOOOooo

"I knew that night had been a mistake." Lauren Holt wouldn't sit down. She paced my living room, her eyes jerking wildly around as she nibbled at her otherwise perfect manicure.

"Normally I'd agree with you, but it gave me my daughters." The girls were asleep in the nursery. Lauren had only agreed to come over if she didn't have to see them. I told her I couldn't promise they wouldn't wake up, but that I'd keep them in their nursery as long as she was there.

Lauren pursed her lips and stared out the window in my kitchen, the same one I looked out hours earlier. It was late, there was no way to see anything out of it, but I don't think it mattered to Lauren.

She turned to me. "We have to come clean. We have to tell them everything, so I can prove I wasn't in Liberty. I didn't have access to my car that night."

"But if we tell them everything, your family will know about the girls."

Lauren flinched as if I'd hit her. "I know, but I can't go to prison. I simply can't."

"Trust me, I can't afford to go to prison either. I have daughters to raise." I refrained from calling them "our daughters" because they weren't. They were mine.

Lauren had birthed them, but she was not their mother. She didn't want to be.

"We need to figure out the next steps. Before we come out about all of this, we need to get everything in place. Your parents cannot come after my girls."

Lauren didn't say anything. She continued staring off into the black expanse.

"This is why I hid from them. I did my part. I did everything I could to protect them." Her voice cracked, and for a second, it sounded like she actually cared about the girls.

I knew, deep down, Lauren only cared about herself. She

was looking out for number one. Children would ruin her dreams of a political career.

"We should have been more careful about the money exchanges," she complained.

"I know that now, but who could have predicted all of this?"

Lauren turned around on her heels. She was an attractive woman, which is why I fell into bed with her a year prior. That and having had too much to drink at the bar. I never asked her the reason she'd slept with me that night. I was just stupid and lonely. But Lauren Holt had an on-again, off-again boyfriend at the time. She didn't need me.

"I could have," Lauren said slowly.

"What do you mean?"

"My father and brother, they..." She closed her eyes as she continued to speak. "They put me up to it. It was supposed to be a scandal in and of itself. You were sleeping with the enemy's daughter. That and they asked me to get some of your DNA. I didn't know why at the time, but now I suspect—"

"You're the reason my DNA was found in James' house and car?" My fists were balled up at my sides. I'd never hit a woman, but damn, I wished she were her brother or father in that moment.

"I had no idea they were going to frame you for murder!"

"What did you think they wanted my damn DNA for Lauren?"

"I don't know. I just wanted my father to be proud of me." Her eyes popped open and there were tears in them. I wasn't sure if they were real or crocodile tears, but the words behind them sounded sincere enough. "He promised me that if we won this election, he'd help further my career. And I'd do anything to make it on my own, Jeremiah. Anything."

"Even frame an innocent man?"

She didn't say anything. She couldn't look at me either.

For months, I'd sent her money. Not because she was poor – she was far from it. But because her own father would suspect something if she touched any of the funds he had access to. And he had access to all her money because Lauren hadn't done much on her own. She was born a Holt and that was all the work she had to do to get rich.

I sent her money to keep up with doctor's appointments, to stay in Tahiti, to sip virgin cocktails to her heart's delight. And for what? For her to frame me for fucking murder.

No, Jeremiah. You did all that for your girls. And you have them. They were worth it.

"Well you're going to do the right thing now, Lauren. You're going to tell the cops everything."

Lauren didn't answer me. She stared at me, and I wasn't sure if I could trust her.

Problem was, she was the only one who could save my ass.

ELLE

"You ou need to talk to him," Josie said, sitting across from me at Smothered in Love diner.

We were grabbing breakfast before I went to the courthouse for Jeremiah's trial. Before I knew it, several weeks had passed. I had been so hurt by him insinuating that I couldn't be trusted, I'd avoided his calls and texts. But I needed to be there for the trial. I needed to know what was going on for the sake of Amelia and Grace. I couldn't avoid him for much longer.

"I was so stupid," I said, staring down at my pancakes. My stomach turned just thinking about eating. Damned morning sickness. "I should handle this on my own."

"And what are you going to do? Keep the baby a secret from him?"

She was right. I couldn't hide it forever. He'd find out eventually. Even if he was behind bars, he'd find out during one of the visits with the girls. I was still their guardian, after all. And the idea of having three babies to care for filled me with fear. It was like a weight was pressing down on me. I'd taken a pregnancy test that morning, which was positive. I was only about three or four weeks along. Even though I couldn't feel the baby inside me, I knew it was there.

And as much as I wanted it, I was scared out of my mind.

It was partially why I had avoided Jeremiah. My period had never come, though I spotted slightly. Josie had told me that was enough, and for a little bit, I believed her. But then it became clear something wasn't right. I took the test to ease my mind, to prove that it was all in my head. But instead, it proved that I was pregnant.

"You need to eat, sweetie," Josie said, reaching across the table and patting my hand.

"My stomach is upset. I'm not sure I can."

Josie raised her hand and called Felicity over. "One ginger ale, please."

Felicity nodded and walked off to get the drink.

"Ginger was my best friend during my pregnancy," Josie confided. "A little ginger ale should soothe the tummy, and from there, eat smaller meals - but you need to make sure you eat."

"I know," I sighed, looking back down at my plate. Pancakes had sounded good when I ordered them, but now they seemed like a very bad idea. So heavy with syrup. I reached for my toast instead, nibbling a bit on it.

"Good girl," Josie said.

Felicity brought over the ginger ale and slipped into the booth beside Josie. "So what's going on?" She rested her face in her hands. "I've been so out of the loop, but I can tell something's wrong, so spill the beans, girls."

Josie looked at me. It was my news to share, and so far, she was the only one who knew. Felicity was one of my closest friends, though, and I was going to need all the support I could get.

"I'm pregnant," I whispered, hoping no one else could hear me.

"What? When did this happen?" Felicity squealed a little too loudly. I hushed her and she apologized before continuing, "So who's the father?"

I cringed. "Jeremiah."

"Wait. Jeremiah Jenkins?"

"I think I'm going to be sick," I stated, wanting any excuse to leave this conversation. But I stayed seated and the feeling passed.

"I take that as a yes," Felicity leaned back into the booth. "Damn. I work too much. I miss everything around here."

I checked my phone, and there was a voicemail from Jeremiah. My finger hovered over the button to delete it, but I decided not to this time. I wouldn't be calling him back. Especially since he had to be at the courthouse soon. It wasn't the time to talk to him.

But if not now, when? What if he got convicted and went to prison?

Don't think like that, Elle.

"What was that?" I pulled myself back to the conversation.

Felicity and Josie were giggling about something.

"Nothing, just saying that I'm the last one in our friend group without a family," Felicity sighed. "That's what I get for being a workaholic I guess."

There was some sadness in Felicity's eyes. A bit of jealousy too. Not that she had any reason to be jealous. The father of my child might end up behind bars; I might be a single mother to not one, but three children under the age of two.

"I better go," I said, pushing my chair back.

"Oh, breakfast is on me," Felicity said, waving it off. "Consider it a congratulations gift."

"I don't think there is such a thing."

"There is now. Go, get your baby daddy free and start your family."

Felicity patted my arm and offered one of her sweet smiles. She had such a good heart; I hoped she'd get her own family one day. And I prayed things worked out better for her than they were for me right now.

Ooo000ooo

I slipped into a seat near the back of the courtroom just as the proceedings were starting. I'd sat in on cases before, but always for work. This was far more personal. I wouldn't be covering the trial. Lucy was there, sitting a few rows up from me. This was her beat, and I let her cover it. I had personally decided to stop writing about Jeremiah altogether. I should have avoided it from the beginning, but I was even closer to it all now - and everyone was right. I could be biased.

Plus, I didn't want to divulge anything that Jeremiah had shared with me in confidence. He already didn't trust me; I didn't want to give him any more reasons to not confide in me.

We were going to have a baby together, after all.

I took a deep breath as they read their opening statements.

Most of it was a blur. A bureaucratic dance that was similar in most court cases. But then Jeremiah took the stand.

He looked tired, older than usual with bags under his eyes and lines deep in his brow from frowning. But he was still as gorgeous as I remembered him to be growing up. His dark hair was brushed nicely. The greys at his temples seemed to have multiplied since I'd last seen him. There seemed to be more in his beard too, which was trimmed nicely, as always.

I could count on one hand the number of times he'd worn a suit. My father's funeral was one of those times. While he looked hot as hell in his usual jeans and casual wear, I had to admit, a suit fit him nicely too. It was all black, Jeremiah's favorite color to wear. Black jacket. Black shirt. And a black tie that had some small details on it that I couldn't make out from this distance.

His eyes met mine from where he was sitting. He raised an eyebrow; maybe he was surprised I was there. I couldn't tell.

I wanted to be there for him. Even after the fight, I wanted there to be an *us*. I just wasn't sure how it would be possible if he didn't trust me.

His lawyer brought up the deposits from his account.

"Can you explain why you were sending Lauren Holt large sums of money, at least once a month, for ten months out of the last year?"

"Yes," Jeremiah said, clearing his throat. He looked away from me as he finished speaking. "Lauren is the mother of my daughters. We had a one-night stand. She got pregnant but didn't want to be a mother. I sent her money to support her during that time."

After the judged quieted the gasps and murmurings in the room, Sam continued. "Lauren Holt needed financial support?" Sam asked.

"She didn't need it, but she didn't want to use her father's money since she didn't want her parents to know about the babies."

Tears welled in my eyes. Such a simple response, one I'd have believed had he told me. Had he trusted me enough to talk to me.

If I were raising his girls, I had a right to know who their mother was. I had a right to now that the Holts could be a threat to them. But Jeremiah had withheld that critical information from me because he thought I'd splash it across the front page of the newspaper as if I lacked any sort of integrity.

"Why didn't you tell anyone about this before?" Sam asked, facing the jury.

"Because like I said, Lauren didn't want her parents to know. She was afraid they may try to come after the girls. I was worried about that too. I wanted to protect my daughters."

"So you told no one?"

"No one. I couldn't trust anyone to keep this secret. I'm only talking about it now because I'm under oath."

"And Lauren, where was she the night of James Fitzhenry's disappearance?"

"She was at the hospital, having just given birth to the girls."

My heart stopped, and it felt like I couldn't breathe. When I mentioned Lauren's car, the reason he knew it wasn't her had nothing to do with the witness not being reliable - he knew where she was that night and had lied to me.

The rest of the testimony was a blur, and the tears continued to fall down my cheeks. I tried to hide them, but when it became too hard, I stood up and hurried out of the courtroom. I ran to the bathroom, where I locked myself in a stall and cried for what felt like an eternity.

"Elle?" A knock came at the bathroom door. Jeremiah. "Are you in there?"

I didn't answer.

"One of the guards saw you go in here, so I know you are," he said through the door. "We're on recess, but I only have a few minutes. Please talk to me."

I needed to talk to him. I'd have to face him eventually. I was having his baby. With a deep sigh, I exited the restroom.

When the door opened, Jeremiah seemed surprised, as if he hadn't expected me to come out.

"Elle, I'm sorry I didn't tell you everything. I just had to be careful, for the girls' sake. I made a deal with Lauren not to tell anyone."

"You asked me to raise your girls, Jeremiah. Don't you think this is information they'd want to know someday? That I should know? Just in case the Holts came after them or something?"

"I know. I didn't think it would come to this," Jeremiah said.

"You should have trusted me."

"I do trust you, Elle. In the beginning, I wasn't sure," he said honestly, earnestly. "You had a tendency to write about anything you found newsworthy."

"Wait, you're still mad at me for the article I wrote about you?"

"Not mad, but it made me hesitate sharing things with you."

"I'd never put the girls in danger, Jeremiah. I would never betray you, not even for my career." I felt cornered, with him standing in front of me. I needed fresh air, and I needed it fast. I pushed past him, but he grabbed my arm. I pulled my arm free and glared at him.

"Elle, please."

"You need to trust me, Jeremiah. Because whether you like it or not, we're going to be connected whether you go to prison or not."

"What are you talking about?"

I closed my eyes and spit out the words. "I'm pregnant."

"What? How did this— Weren't you on the pill?"

My eyes popped open. "You know, it takes two to tango, right? It's not just my doing here."

Except it was. I blamed myself. He still should have worn a condom, but I should have said something.

"You're right, I shouldn't have assumed, it's just—" Jeremiah stammered. "I can't do this right now, Elle."

"Can't do what? Father three children?" I asked, my voice hard. "Because like it or not, it's happening."

"Elle, I can't."

I burst into tears. This was not how I wanted it to go. I had wanted him to be happy, but I fucked up. It wasn't the right time, but like it or not, it was happening.

"Well, I have to deal with it. You can check out, but I can't." I needed air. My stomach roiled, and I was sweating profusely. I was going to be sick without air. I stormed away, heading for the exit.

"Elle, come back!"

Jeremiah chased me to the front doors, but in the distance, I heard his lawyer's voice calling him back.

The recess was over. He had to return to the trial.

I stepped outside, and the cool air felt good on my skin. I closed my eyes, breathing in and out, remembering some of Josie's relaxation techniques.

My emotions were crazy these days, and I blamed the hormones. I was a mess. I shouldn't have told him like that. What had I expected?

JEREMIAH

I'd fucked up with Elle. I had reacted badly. But she had completely blindsided me at the worst possible time. I was fighting for my freedom and she just blurted it out in the hallway.

As soon the trial was over for the day, I tried to call her.

No answer.

As usual.

There were several missed calls - some from Lauren. Others from numbers I didn't recognize at first.

I listened to the voicemail from Lauren. She hadn't gone to the police, and like Elle, she'd avoided my calls since the night I talked to her in my home.

"Well it's out now. My parents heard that Amelia and Grace are my daughters, thanks to the press. I've left town temporarily, but be warned - they aren't going to let this go. And to answer your previous questions, I am not going to turn on my family. I'm sorry. I'm not strong enough to do that."

The line went dead. With dread, I pulled up the next voicemail.

"Hello, this is Vincent Barry, I'm George Holt's attorney. I'm calling to discuss George's granddaughters, Amelia and Grace Jenkins. Please give me a call at your earliest convenience."

Damn. I stood on the steps of the courthouse, fear running through my veins. I stared off in the distance, not even realizing the voicemail had ended until the next one began.

It was George himself. "Think you can hide my grand-daughters from me, huh? Lauren may have had a moment of selfishness, but she will come to her senses, you can count on that. Those girls will be raised by their mother."

The line went dead again. I stopped the voicemails. I'd heard enough. I had to get to my girls. Then I'd talk to Sam. There was no way Lauren's family would take them away from me. I wouldn't let those monsters near my children.

Liberty being as small as it was, the daycare wasn't very far from the courthouse. I still drove there as quickly as I could, not wanting to carry the girls in the cold if I could help it. I parked in the lot and hopped from the car.

Right away, my gaze fell on a red Porsche parked near the entrance.

Oh hell no, I thought. Only family in Liberty that drove cars like that were the Holts. I knew Piper would never hand over my girls to someone other than me, but I also knew George and Alex were big men.

I quickened my pace, and as I approached the Porsche, the door swung open, nearly hitting me. George Holt stepped out of the passenger side. His son, Alex, had been behind the wheel.

My girls weren't in the car as far as I could tell. That was a relief.

"What are you doing here?" I growled.

"I'm here to see my granddaughters," George said with a

smirk. "Maybe take them home, if you've come to your senses and realize they belong with their mother."

"Never." I clenched my fists at my side.

George laughed. "We'll let the court decide that, and let's face it - you might have money, but you have nothing compared to us."

"Money can't buy you everything. Not in Liberty," I said, walking up to George and standing an inch of him. I felt his breath against my face. He didn't move back. "Your reputation precedes you. And once the truth comes out about the bribes, your family is the one going down. You'll be the ones in cuffs and orange jumpsuits."

George reared his head back and cackled. "Do you hear that, Alex? Jeremiah thinks we're going to prison."

"You will. Mark my word. Your wife was already seen accepting bribes and—"

"Elizabeth? Dear, old Elizabeth accepting bribes?"" George chuckled and rubbed his face. "No, we've already cleared that up. Brody even spoke to the police on our behalf. Brody purchased some antique chairs from my wife and was merely paying for them. We have the receipts and everything to back it up."

"Why would you meet in an alley after dark to exchange money for antique chairs?"

"That alley is also where people park when they visit the local shops, isn't it?"

"The shops were closed. It was eleven at night."

"The diner was still open, and Elizabeth had popped in to pick up a salad she really loves. Since she was in the area, she decided to meet Brody. It's all innocent."

"Bullshit." I knew a lie when I heard one. It sounded like a good one, but there were holes in his story. Too many holes. Like why would Elizabeth drive herself into town? She often had staff pick up things like that for her. But I knew no matter what questions I asked, George would have an explanation. They'd worked on their story, and Brody was working with them.

The question was, did the police buy it? Since I hadn't heard of any arrests, apparently they'd worked something out.

Dammit, Lauren. I need you to go to the police, I thought to myself.

George continued smirking and I wanted to punch that smirk right off his face.

"Is there a problem here?" A man's voice spoke from behind me.

I turned to find Grant Barnes, Piper's husband and the owner of the property, standing behind us. He was a good guy, ex-military, a friend of Elle's growing up as well.

"Not at all," George said, backing away from me. "I was just leaving."

George climbed into his Porsche, but before closing the door, he offered some parting words. "I will see my granddaughters, Jeremiah. One way or another. I will see them, and they will be coming home with me shortly."

He slammed the door, and the car sped off. I watched it as it left the parking lot, my blood boiling. I was relieved that they were gone but worried about what the future might hold.

"What was that about?" Grant asked.

"I guess you haven't heard the news?"

"Nope. Don't really keep up with the news or gossip really."

Probably the only person in Liberty who hadn't heard yet.

"Don't worry, you'll hear about it before long," I muttered. I marched into the daycare. I wasn't about to waste any more time talking.

I needed to get my girls and take them home where they belonged.

Ooo000ooo

"Lauren, please call me back. We have to talk."

Dammit, Lauren. She'd left town, leaving me to handle this.

Amelia and Grace were on the floor beside me. I didn't want to leave their side; I was even thinking of moving their cribs to my room. If I ever managed to sleep. I closed my eyes, feeling the weight of everything. My phone rang, and I wasn't sure if I hoped more for Elle or Lauren to be calling me back.

"Jeremiah, I told you - I'm not dealing with this. It's your problem, not mine," Lauren said without a greeting.

"Your dad is threatening to take the girls away."

Lauren was quiet for a long time. "I don't know what to tell you. This is why I was worried about having them. They'd have been better off if I'd—"

"Stop it. Don't you dare say it."

I stared at their sweet faces. Grace lifted her head and offered a few gurgles and a smile. Amelia gripped the handle of a rattle in front of her, her eyes staring at it like it was the greatest thing ever.

My heart broke for my babies. So sweet. So innocent. They deserved better than this mess.

"Jeremiah, I can't do anything. Just be careful, because my parents will stop at nothing to get what they want."

"Thanks for telling me what I already know." I helped Amelia with the rattle, helping her shake it. Her eyes lit up when she heard the sound it made. "You're really not going to do anything? What if they call you to the stand, would you lie and commit perjury about what your parents put you up to?"

"I won't turn on my family, Jeremiah. I can't."

"So that's a yes? You'd commit perjury for them? After everything they've done to you."

"Goodbye, Jeremiah. Please don't call me again."

The line went dead.

Shit.

I tried Elle again. No answer. Straight to voicemail.

"Elle, please listen to me. I'm sorry, for everything. I'm sorry about how I reacted. It was just a shock to me. I was terrified to be the father of two children, and to find out I'm going to be a dad to another one? Well, it scared me, but—"

There was a beep signalling that my message was cut off. I had the opportunity to re-record it or delete it.

I deleted it. She wouldn't listen to it anyway, and it had been a mess. It likely would have made things worse. I needed to get my shit together, form a coherent thought. But with everything going on, I wasn't sure if that would happen anytime soon.

ELLE

I pushed the grilled chicken around on my plate. I couldn't
blame morning sickness for my loss of appetite today. It
was lunch time, and I was sitting in Smothered in Love by
myself. I sat by the window, watching the people pass by. A
couple with two little kids walked by, all of them bundled up
in their winter clothing. They held tiny cups of hot chocolate
they'd picked up down the street at the bakery.

I wanted a happy family like that so badly.

Instead, I was sitting in a booth, pregnant and alone, my
emotions getting the best of me and my food going to waste.

I hadn't felt like eating since the run-in with Jeremiah.

I looked down at my plate, managed to take a few bites as
the family passed by and out of sight. I looked out again and
saw a familiar face. I don't know what got into me, but I
pushed myself out of my seat and out the door. I walked past
the black Jaguar with the ridiculous vanity plates.

Lauren Holt was standing on the sidewalk, putting some
change into a meter and cursing to herself. She looked tired.

"Hey, I heard you left town," I called out. "Decided to
come back and see your girls?"

Lauren looked up, eyes wide. "Elle, what—"

"Oh, wait, that's right. You want nothing to do with them. I don't know how a mother could just throw her children away like that. Put them up for adoption, sure, but you know where they're at, you know Jeremiah could end up behind bars, yet you do nothing." My voice was shaking with rage.

"Elle, please," she said, her voice cracking. For a second, I almost felt bad for her, but she stiffened her spine. "You have no idea what you're talking about," she spat. "You should just go back inside the restaurant before you make a fool of yourself."

"You should do something about your family," I seethed, my hatred clear in my voice. "I heard they want to take the babies away from Jeremiah. You can't let that happen."

Lauren's face blanched. "I told Jeremiah I can't help him."

"If he goes to prison, you really want your father raising those girls?"

Lauren opened her mouth to speak, but then closed it. She no longer looked me in the eye. Disgusted, I said, "Yeah, I didn't think so. But if you don't do something, it very well could be your dad - and dare I say it, your brother - raising those babies, and we both know how terrible they are."

I didn't want to say it, but I could see the broken woman behind the façade. The drinking during the interview, the way she acted around her father and brother, it was clear she had been damaged by them. Maybe she wouldn't have been a half bad person had her family not stuck their claws in her.

"There's nothing I can do," she reiterated, and for the first time in her life, she sounded helpless. The rich and powerful Lauren Holt was nearly whimpering. "I can't speak against them. I can't."

"I know somewhere inside, you care about those girls. You wouldn't have carried them for nine months, given birth to them, and made sure they were cared for if you didn't. I want to believe part of you loves them, even if you try so hard not to."

My own baby wasn't even the size of a soybean, and I loved him or her more than life itself. I couldn't imagine carrying my child for nine months and not loving it. Even giving the girls to Jeremiah to raise was an act of love.

Lauren still wouldn't meet my gaze, but I saw the tears sliding down her cheeks. I'd hit on something, that much was clear. I just prayed it was enough to make her do the right thing. Because we were running out of time.

"You're right. There's no way my dad can get near those girls. Not after what he's done to me." She stopped there, but I didn't need to hear more.

I already knew there must have been abuse. Whether it be mental or physical, I could see it all over Lauren's face. Her father had hurt her. And I had to believe she wouldn't let him do it to those girls.

"I have to go," she said abruptly, turning away from me and hurrying down the street.

I waited, debating on going back inside to finish my chicken salad. But I decided against it. I had to see where she was going and why she dared come back into town. She was probably better off staying far away from the mess, but something had brought her back to Liberty.

I kept my distance from her and watched as she turned down an alley. I waited and then turned down as well, ducking behind a dumpster. I could hear Lauren talking to her brother. No, not talking. She was yelling. She was screaming.

"I can't do this anymore, Alex. I'm done."

"What are you going to do, Lauren? Run to the cops?" Alex scoffed.

I glanced around the side. Lauren was pacing, her arms

wrapped around her as if to warm herself or to protect herself.

"You and dad set me up. I wanted to shame Jeremiah, not frame him for murder. It's gone too far," she pronounced.

"Your car was in front of James' place that night, Lauren. If anyone is going down for the crime, it's you. I made sure of it."

"Yeah, well, I have an alibi, Alex." Lauren stopped in front of her brother and stared him directly in the eye. "I was in the hospital giving birth to the twins, and I stayed there for several days. I have proof. I have witnesses. You have nothing."

Alex raised his hand, and the slapping sound echoed throughout the alley. I jumped, covering my mouth to avoid making a sound. Lauren stood her ground, her hand rubbing her cheek.

"You can't continue bullying me forever. I used to have nothing to lose, but that's changed now. I will do whatever I need to in order to protect my children."

Alex lunged toward her, grabbing her by the shoulders and pressing her into the wall. "You won't live long enough to talk to the cops."

My heart stopped. A coughing sound caught my attention, and I turned to the end of the alley to find Abe Hammond, world-renowned doctor and a very respected member of our community standing at the end.

"Is there a problem here?" he asked.

Alex let go of Lauren. "No," he said, storming off toward the end of the alley. He stopped and turned to Lauren. "But there will be if you talk. Don't be stupid, Lauren."

Alex hurried towards my end of the alley, passing by the dumpster close enough that I could have reached out and touched him. I pressed against the back, and Abe's eyes met mine. He saw me, but I knew my secret was safe with him.

DADDY'S BEST FRIEND | 181

He walked down the alley toward Lauren, and I knew she was safe. She was in good hands - a doctor's hands. I hurried out of there as quickly as I could, making sure to watch for Alex.

I returned to the diner and stopped outside. My head was spinning. I didn't know what to do. Should I go back inside, pretend that everything was normal and finish my lunch - if it was still there? I looked around, careful to watch for Alex or any of the Holts.

Lauren came out of the alley with Dr. Hammond, and she saw me standing in front of the diner. We shared a look. I didn't know if she knew I was there, listening in. Mascara stained her pale cheeks. She'd been crying. Her cheek where Alex had slapped her was bright red and would likely bruise. And she had witnesses to all of it.

As the two of them walked down the street toward Lauren's car, she stopped. "I'll go to the cops," she muttered. "I'll head there now."

"Thank you. You're doing the right thing," I whispered.

She didn't look at me, she just stared at the ground, but she nodded.

It would soon be over. The Holts would go to jail. Jeremiah was safe. And his girls would have their father. I prayed it would turn out that way.

JEREMIAH

When someone knocked on my door, I prayed it was Elle. She still wasn't speaking to me, but we needed to talk. I needed to apologize and make things right.

But when I opened the door, dread set in. "Teddy? What are you doing here?"

"May I come in, Jeremiah?" The sheriff just had that look about him - he had bad news.

My heart sank, and I feared the worst. "Is it Elle?" I asked him, my legs turning to jelly at the very thought. I stepped back to let him enter, closing the door behind him.

"No, as far as I know, Elle is fine."

Relief washed over me. Knowing that, I could walk again. I led Teddy down the hallway and into the dining room. "Would you like a beer?"

"I'm working, I can't," Teddy said.

"Coffee then?"

"No, I'm fine," Teddy said. "Have a seat, Jeremiah."

I was antsy. Even knowing Elle was fine, something was obviously wrong. I nodded and took a seat across from Teddy, trying to prepare for the news.

"Look, there's no easy way to say this, so I'm just going to come out with it. Lauren Holt was found dead earlier this evening."

The news hit me hard, and I leaned back in my chair, at a loss for words. Teddy let the news sink in, as I went through a series of emotions. She was the twins' mother. Even if she was fairly awful at times, she was still a person.

"Damn. What happened?" I asked.

"She was shot in the back of the head. We found her in her car, not too far from here. Someone reported a gunshot, but no one saw anything."

I had a pretty good idea who was behind it.

"Jeremiah, I know she was the mother of your twins, so I expect this news is hard for you, but I have to ask - where were you between 5pm and 7pm this evening?"

"I was here, with my daughters," I said. "You can't possibly think...No way, not this again. I didn't kill her."

Teddy held his hands up. "I have to investigate all angles, Jeremiah. Please understand it's nothing personal."

I wiped at my face as if I could wipe the whole fucking nightmare away. I stared at Teddy, trying to piece everything together. "Have you talked to her family yet? Do they have alibis?"

Teddy sighed. "We're talking to them now."

Yeah, I was sure they'd paid for some alibis. They always managed to find a way to prove their innocence, no matter the crime. I gripped the corner of the table so hard I feared I might crack the wood.

I sighed, furious and saddened at the same time. "I'm not going to answer another question without a lawyer present."

"I understand," Teddy said, standing. "I'd encourage you to give him a call. I'm sure we'll be in touch."

I walked Teddy to the door and leaned against it, cursing everything in the world. The only good thing to have come out of all this were my girls. And Elle. But she wasn't talking to me right now. She had my child growing inside her - another child who might grow up without a father because of this shitshow.

There was another knock on the door, and I swung it open. "Teddy, I told you—"

I stopped when I saw Elle, wrapped in a wool coat and her hair windblown. Her mascara ran down her cheeks.

"Oh Jeremiah, I heard the news."

She rushed into my arms before I knew what hit me. I held her, still trying to decide if it was real. Her sobs were very real.

Between gasping and crying, Elle managed to get out, "It's her brother. I know it is. I saw them—"

"You saw them?"

She calmed down, hiccupping from all the crying. "Yes, and so did Dr. Hammond," she continued. "We have witnesses to prove that Alex threatened Lauren."

"But you know the Holts, Elle. They will find a way to get around this."

"We have to try, Jeremiah," she insisted, taking my hand in hers. I brought my other hand to her face, to wipe the tears from her cheeks. God, she was so beautiful. Inside and out.

"Elle, we need to talk about the baby."

A pained look crossed her face. "I know it's a lot to handle, Jeremiah. I can raise the baby on my own if needed, but—"

"No, you won't. I mean, unless I end up behind bars. But as long as I'm a free man, we will raise that child together. We will be a family."

Elle raised her face to look at me, and more tears pooling in her eyes and falling. But these weren't sad tears. "Oh Jeremiah," she croaked. "That's all I want. Just for us to be a family."

I lifted her chin and pressed my lips to her. "I want that too."

I wasn't sure if we'd get our happy ending, considering our circumstances currently. But I wanted her to be with me forever. I wanted to be there for all my children. And the idea of having a child with her, of giving Grace and Amelia a sibling, actually filled me with excitement - once I got past the initial fear.

"I'm sorry I reacted the way I did. It was a shock and I didn't know how to process it."

"I shouldn't have told you like that," Elle said at the same time.

I leaned into her, our foreheads touching. "It's scary thinking I might not be there for my children."

"You will be, Jeremiah," she said, her voice impassioned, taking my hands in hers. "I'll tell the cops everything I know, and I'm sure Doc Hammond will do the same. He's a good man."

"I just hope it's enough."

"It has to be."

We were silent for a long time, standing in the front hall-way, holding each other. When I realized she was still all bundled up from being outside, I stepped back.

"Oh God, come in," I said. "Let me take your coat."

I slipped the coat off, and even though it was too soon, my eyes fell on her belly. My child was in there, growing. Soon, she'd be showing and the whole world would know. The idea of her carrying my baby turned me on more than I expected it to. Once I hung up her coat, I kissed her deeply, and we moved to the couch.

The girls were asleep, we had the living room to ourselves, and it was clear we wouldn't make it to the bedroom. I stripped her down, her clothes falling as we moved across the room.

She was just as turned on, obviously. She stripped me down, her hands fumbling with my belt, then my zipper. She slid my pants over my hips and dropped to her knees in front of me.

Her big, brown eyes stared up at me, her mouth open. Her perfect pink tongue darted out and teased the tip of my cock. She licked the precum, then took me inside her hot, wet mouth, though she couldn't take me all the way. Her hand made up the difference, moving up and down as her mouth sucked and licked.

My hands were tangled in her soft, silky hair. I'd never met anyone as beautiful as her. I felt like the luckiest man in the world as she sucked my cock, bringing me very close to the edge.

I pulled her back, gently tugging at her hair. "Stop," I groaned. "To the couch."

She followed me, and together, we fell to the couch. She was in my lap, straddling me, her breasts free and bouncy as she moved, grinding against me.

I grabbed my cock and guided it into her, watching the look on her face as I entered her. Her eyes popped open wide; her head fell forward. She rested it against my chest, feeling me deep inside of her. She was so tight, gripping my cock so snugly with her lips. I could stay like that forever, savoring the warm, velvety wetness of her pussy, but she slowly began rocking back and forth.

She raised her head, and I kissed her deeply, gripping her hips and helping guide her.

This is Heaven, I thought. Fucking the woman I loved, who was pregnant with my child. It was everything I'd always wanted, and my dream girl had been in front of me for so long.

I'm glad I finally stopped fighting my destiny.

ELLE

I stared deep in his eyes as I rode him, our bodies united as one. His beard brushed against my cheek, sending chills down my spine. His hands moved up and down my hips, stroking my skin with those rough hands.

It didn't take long for me to reach climax, my entire body tightening around him, my pussy clenching around his cock as I came.

"Yes, yes, cum for me, baby," he whispered into my ear, his breath warm against my flesh.

He knew my body well; he knew I was orgasming without me even telling him. And from the look on his face, he enjoyed it as much as he did his own, doing everything he could to extend it - to make it last as long as possible.

And once my orgasm ended, I collapsed on top of him, but Jeremiah wasn't done with me. No, I never just came once with him. He always made sure I came multiple times. No man had treated me to so many in one session, but Jeremiah wasn't like most men. I'd known that my entire life, and now I witnessed it for myself.

He rolled us over, hovering above me on the couch. He

slipped his cock free from my pussy and moved down my body, kissing every inch of my belly. Soon, my belly would be growing, no longer flat but full with his child.

He kissed it lovingly, and I thought I might melt.

Then he moved lower, spread my thighs open, and kissed me in my most intimate spot. His tongue darted in and out of my pussy, licking up all the juices from my orgasm. I was so wet, and he was only making me wetter.

"Oh God," I cried as he teased my clit. "Don't stop, please. Don't stop."

He kept at it, my hands in his hair, pulling him to me as I came for a second time - my body spasming and writhing underneath him, nearly taking us both off the couch. My thighs quivered until I couldn't take it anymore.

Yanking his hair, I pulled him back up to me. He situated us so I was lying flat and he was hovering above me again. He thrust into me, our bodies crashing together once more. It felt so natural, so perfect, as if we were always meant to be together.

Jeremiah fucked me with desperation. His face contorted and twisted in a look of pleasure as he buried himself inside me over and over again.

He held onto the arm of the couch and thrust into me one last time - burying his shaft as deep as it would possibly go. A deep growl escaped his chest as I felt him cumming inside me.

And I came too, thinking about how he'd filled me with his seed and impregnated me. It was the sexiest, most intimate feeling in the world - being with the man who had given me a child, knowing that he loved me and would care for me.

Jeremiah collapsed on top of me, hardly holding himself up. We were as close as two people could be.

He stared deep into my eyes. "I love you, Elle. I love you so fucking much."

"I love you too, Jeremiah."

He kissed me then slipped his deflated cock out of me. "Please tell me you're staying the night," he said.

"I wouldn't have it any other way."

Ooo000ooo

I awoke to the sound of Jeremiah's phone. I knew we had to be up early for the trial. I assumed it was his alarm, but heard Jeremiah mutter, "Give me a second."

I rolled over and found Jeremiah climbing from bed, talking on the phone. "Yeah, yeah, I can be there," he said. He hung up and placed the phone on the end table beside the bed.

"Who was it?" I asked, rubbing my eyes.

"It's Sam. Says he wants to meet before the trial this morning. He has some news."

Jeremiah looked at me, and I could tell he was worried. I was too. "Did he say if the news was good or bad?"

"I didn't ask him. I assume it has to be bad. I haven't had good news in a while."

I rolled over to the edge of the bed and reached for him. Jeremiah dropped to his knees to be at my level. He kissed the tip of my nose, then my forehead, then my lips.

"Whatever happens, we will get through it," I whispered.

"I hope so, Elle," he said softly. "I need to get ready."

"I'm going with you," I announced, flipping my legs around until I was sitting.

Jeremiah didn't argue. I guess he'd finally learned it was

useless to argue with me. Or maybe he didn't want to be alone. Either way, I was going with him.

I helped him feed the babies, and we sat mostly in silence - worried about the fate today would bring. Perhaps there'd be more charges for Lauren's death - even though I knew Jeremiah didn't kill her. I'd go to the police with what I knew. I'd also head over to Dr. Hammond's office and see if he'd go with me. I made these plans in my head as we hurried through the rest of the morning routine.

God, when we have three, it will be even harder, I thought. But we'd make do.

We got the girls buckled in Jeremiah's truck and headed toward town.

I took his hand. "It's going to be okay."

"I sure hope so."

I noticed he glanced in the rear-view mirror a few times, watching something in it. I turned around and saw a black car on our tail. Frowning, I said, "What a jerk."

Jeremiah didn't say anything, he just kept checking the mirror, both hands firmly on the wheel. "Hold on," he said. "I'm going to pull over and let them pass."

He pulled over to the side of the narrow road, and we waited. No car passed. I was about to turn back around to check what was happening, but Jeremiah slammed on the gas and sped off.

"What's going on?"

"It's Alex," he said.

"How do you know?" I looked behind me, and the black car was back on our ass, and I noticed the license plates.

RenRox.

Shit.

Lauren was dead. It couldn't be her.

"What's he doing?"

"I don't know, but whatever it is, it isn't good. We need to get into town," Jeremiah said. "I'm heading to the police station."

We had to get to the end of this road, then head onto the main stretch. It was about two miles after that. Not too far, but with a crazed man on our ass, it felt like an eternity.

The streets were white with a fresh layer of snow too. If things weren't bad enough, the roads weren't clear.

The girls must have sensed our tension; they both started screaming at the top of their lungs. Jeremiah clenched the wheel tightly, reminded that it wasn't just the two of us at risk here - but our children. He turned onto the main road, and the car was right on our heels. He continued speeding down the road when there was a loud pop followed by another.

"Shit," he cursed, zigzagging the vehicle.

"What is it? What are you doing?"

"He's shooting at our tires."

Another large pop, much bigger than the others, and the truck swerved uncontrollably. I thought he might have succeeded in hitting our tire. A loud rubbing sound followed, of metal on pavement, but Jeremiah didn't stop.

We could see the lights of town in the distance. We were so close.

Jeremiah straightened the truck and continued toward town. We couldn't stop. Because if we did, we had a pretty good idea of what fate awaited us.

The same as Lauren's.

The same as James'.

But we had more to lose: the girls and the child inside me. Jeremiah drove like his life depended on it, and once we were within city limits, I thought Alex might drive off. But he didn't. He pulled into the police station with us.

"Shit, is he crazy?" Jeremiah muttered.

A sheriff's deputy was getting out of a car when we pulled

in. I knew the guy; his name was Henry. Jeremiah pulled the truck up beside Henry and was about to get out when another loud explosion rocked through the air.

"Jesus, don't look," Jeremiah said, pushing my head down below the windows.

"What? What happened?"

"He shot Henry."

Shit.

My heart raced. Alex was clearly unhinged if he shot a cop in broad daylight.

"Come on out," Alex shouted, taunting us. "I've got nothing else to lose. Might as well finish the job myself."

I looked at Jeremiah. "What's he—"

"I don't know, but there's bound to be cops. We're at—"

Gunshots rang out around us. Glass shattered as our windows exploded. The girls screamed, and I feared the glass, or worse, a stray bullet, would hurt them.

Jeremiah yelled, "Stay down!" and climbed into the back with them, literally shielding their little bodies with his.

I did as I was told and stayed down. The window nearest me exploded, and I screamed as my shoulder screamed in pain and blood began to flow.

Lots of blood.

And then silence, except for the girl's crying.

No more gunshots. Nothing.

Jeremiah raised his head and looked out the back window. I was scared for him, afraid he might get shot - but he said, "Alex is down. Teddy's guys got him." He turned back toward me and saw the blood. "Jesus, Elle!"

"I think—I think I've been shot."

JEREMIAH

Elle's face was pale as the snow outside our window. She appeared to be in shock. When the EMTs arrived, I wanted nothing more than to climb inside the ambulance with her, but she reminded me, "The babies. Take care of them, talk to the cops, then meet me at the hospital."

The EMTs had to pull her hand from mine as they lifted her into the ambulance. I still had no idea what had happened. Alex was dead, so he wasn't talking. And the cops hadn't explained a damn thing to me yet.

My girls were also being checked out by EMTs. They were fine, surprisingly. No glass had hit them, nothing. I'd managed to protect them.

But not Elle.

"She's going to be fine," Teddy said, patting me on the back. "The EMTs said the bullet didn't penetrate, just grazed her arm."

I'd heard that too, but it didn't make me feel much better. If something had happened to Elle or our baby…Jesus, I couldn't even think about that.

"Come on, we'll get you out of here quickly."

Teddy helped me with one of the girls, and we went inside. He gave us a private room. Out of habit, I said, "I'm not talking until my lawyer gets here."

"Relax," Teddy said, taking the seat across from me. "You've been cleared of all charges. We know everything."

I stared at him, astonished. "What? How?"

"Before Lauren was killed, she spoke to Agent Dickinson. She told him everything. They followed up with the leads, figured it all out. George and Elizabeth are currently behind bars for the foreseeable future. But we couldn't find Alex until now."

That's what he'd meant when he'd said he had nothing left to lose. It had been over for him, but he'd wanted to take us with him. He almost succeeded.

It felt like the air had left the room. I couldn't breathe for a moment. I was relieved, so relieved, but it was hard to feel anything but shaken up after everything that had happened.

And Elle was hurt. My girls could have been hurt.

But they weren't. Thank God, everyone survived.

"You know everything?"

"Yep. Lauren had proof too. Had she talked to me directly, well, I would have probably offered her our protection, but the Feds, they don't have our small-town values, I guess. She didn't ask. Not sure why, but she didn't ask and told Dickinson she could handle herself."

It almost sounded like she knew it was over. She went down with her family. She knew once they went down, it wouldn't be long before she did too.

"Oh, and it was James who was working with the Holts and the Pearsons. He was the one taking bribes. Explains the new house, new car, and the vacation, I guess. It was all set up from the beginning to look like it was you, though. They were good. Thorough."

"Not good enough, I guess."

"They were doing this to ruin your name, to take the mayor's seat. And the Pearsons were just being used - they had bigger developers in the wings ready to swoop in when he took office, ready to develop the land for the lithium in our soil."

"I wish I could say I'm surprised, but…"

"I know, I know," Teddy sighed. "Listen, I believed you, Jeremiah. I knew you weren't the type of man to do the things you were accused of, but that's why the Feds got called in. Because we were too close to the case."

I nodded. "It's not your fault, Teddy. I know your hands were tied, but I'm free now? I can go?"

Teddy nodded. "I can give you a ride to the hospital if you'd like."

"As much as I appreciate that, Teddy, I think I've seen the inside of a cop's car a few too many times already."

He chuckled. "Can't say I blame you there."

I'd have to call someone to come pick me up. My truck wasn't going anywhere for a while.

Teddy left the room and I picked up the phone. There was someone I had to call.

"Mrs. Schaeffer? It's Jeremiah." I cringed, hating to be the one to tell her about her daughter ending up in the hospital - but we needed to do it at some point.

We had a lot of news to break to her; this was only just the beginning.

Ooo000ooo

"Oh my sweet Ellie bean," Pamela cried, rushing to her daughter's side.

I stood back, holding the twins close. There was no way I was letting them out of my sight. The threat was gone, sure, but I couldn't imagine wanting to be more than a few feet from them for a while. I wasn't sure if I'd ever be okay with that again. *Poor girls*, I thought. *They're going to have one protective ass dad.* Probably would have been regardless, but when you're nearly driven off the road by a psychopath with your family inside, well, it's easy to feel a little more nervous than usual.

I hadn't told Pamela I was involved with her daughter. I also hadn't told her Elle was pregnant. Those were things we'd tell her together.

Josie was at Elle's side and moved to let Pamela get closer to her.

She seemed to be fine. She was no longer pale. There was no more blood soaking through her shirt. She was in a hospital gown and her arm was wrapped in gauze. She smiled as we'd entered. Even though they'd told me she would be fine, I had to see for myself.

"What did the doctor say?" I asked.

"He said that I was hit with glass and only grazed by a bullet. We'll probably find the bullet in your seat or something." She let out a nervous chuckle. Not because it was funny, but because after everything we'd been through, the emotions could drive you a bit crazy. I understood that feeling well.

"I'm just glad you're okay," Pamela said. Her eyes moved between us. "But I'm curious, why were you two together so early this morning?"

Elle opened her mouth to answer but seemed to think better. I didn't know how much she wanted to tell her mother right now. She glanced at me and asked, "Should we tell her?"

"I think so," Josie added, reminding us both she was there.

This brought more chuckles and nervous laughter from Elle. She stared down at where her mother's hand was entwined with hers.

"What do you think, Jeremiah?"

"I'm ready to tell her when you are."

"Tell me what?" Pamela looked between the two of us. "Someone better tell me something. I'm starting to panic."

"Oh, no, don't worry Mom," Elle rushed, patting her mother's hands. She took a deep breath, closed her eyes and spit it out. "Jeremiah and I are together."

"Together?"

"Yes, as in we're dating."

Pamela's eyes widened and she stood up, seemingly unsure how to handle that information. Before she could say anything, Elle continued.

"And I'm pregnant with his child."

"You're what?"

"You're going to be a grandmother, Pamela." She looked at me, and at first, I thought I saw anger in her eyes.

"You and Elle? What would—" she stopped. "You know what, I think I know what Carl would say." I cringed, fearing the worst. "He would say as long as you treat her right and you're both happy, that's all that matters." Her eyes met mine. "You were one of his favorite people. I don't see why he would disapprove, once he got over the initial shock."

"Thank you, Pamela."

"So are you excited?" Elle asked, nibbling her lip. "You're going to be a grandma."

Pamela lowered herself into a nearby chair as if she had to sit down. "A grandma? Well, I've always wanted to be a grandmother," she mused. She took Elle's hand and brought it to her lips, kissing it. "I couldn't be happier dear."

I closed the distance between us now, comfortable getting closer to her. I bent down and kissed Elle on the cheek.

"And I bet you didn't think you'd get a happy ending?" Josie said from the doorway.

"No, no we didn't," I said, stroking Elle's cheek. "But I guess someone's looking out for us."

I think we all had a good idea about who that person was. Whether or not Carl would have approved, we'd never know for sure. But I think Pamela was right. I think he'd be happy his daughter was taken care of, and I'd do anything in my power to make sure she was happy.

I'd give her the happy family she wanted.

Because deep down, I wanted it too.

EPILOGUE

ELLE - ABOUT A YEAR LATER

"You're overrun by girls," my mother giggled as she greeted me with a gentle side hug, careful not to smoosh the baby attached to my chest.

Jeremiah had Amelia and Grace, and I had baby Charlotte. We were the proud parents of three adorable little girls. Amelia and Grace were growing so fast at two months past their first birthday. Charlotte was not much older than when I came into the twins' lives. It was almost like having triplets at times, and we certainly had our hands full.

But our hearts were just as full.

Jeremiah had a girl on each hip, but my mother took Charlotte from me, coddling and cooing. She treated all three girls like her granddaughters, and as far as we were concerned, they were our family. They called me mama, and I loved them as much I did my own. One day they would learn about Lauren, when they were old enough. Because even though I didn't like the woman very much, in the end, she did the right thing for everyone. She did what was right for her babies, even though it cost her her life.

I took Amelia from Jeremiah, and he wrapped his free

arm around my waist, dotting a kiss on my forehead as he held me close.

"Mayor Schaeffer, are you ready to go on?" a young staffer asked me.

"Oh, yes, of course," I said, handing Amelia back to her father. She reached for me, wanting me to continue holding her.

"Mama."

"I'll be right back, sweetie. Mama has to go talk to these fine people."

I kissed the tip of her nose and made sure all my girls were fine before heading up to the podium.

I was dedicating a large section of Liberty land at the base and in the mountains as a city park. I was also announcing our conservation efforts to keep the lands pristine and untouched - one of the main points I ran on with my election.

I stepped up to the podium and saw my family smiling back at me.

Josie was there with her husband Cyrus and their children. Other familiar faces too. Piper and Grant, with their little family. Lucy, who had once been my assistant editor and now ran the paper. I'd left her in charge, since being mayor and mother was hard enough. And so no one could accuse me of being biased in my own campaign, not that I had anyone running against me since George Holt was in prison. Felicity was off by herself, near the back, standing outside the doors of her diner. Her property butted up against the new city park land, and she was one of my biggest supporters.

We all loved this town, and now I was in charge of protecting it.

For my family and all of theirs.

My speech was fairly brief, talking about the initiatives

we had planned along with conservation efforts and activities we would bring to Liberty.

I ended the speech with, "I'm dedicated to protecting Liberty, the town we've all lived in and loved. I grew up here, I came back here, and I intend to stay for the rest of my life. I will raise my children here, and while I will support economic growth and development for the small businesses that make our town so special, I will never let that tarnish the beautiful town we call home."

The applause was deafening, and I could see my baby girl starting to fuss from all the noise. I was mayor, but I was also a mom and my family would always come first. They were the reason I discovered my new passion: politics.

I hurried from the stage and scooped Charlotte into my arms, and as soon as she was with her mother, she quieted down.

"She has the magic touch," Jeremiah said with a wink to my mom.

"That she does."

My speech might have been over, but the event was just getting started. People from outside Liberty had also come out to the event, journalists from other parts of Utah and even national papers too.

I'd made a name for myself. Not only from running for mayor, but publishing an article, and later a book, about the Holts and the entire case and how an innocent man had almost gone to prison. It was a cautionary tale for other towns that might be blinded by the money.

And it was a best-seller all over the world.

I'd peaked with my writing career, in my opinion. I turned down offers from *People* and *Time* to write for them - turning my attention to being more active in politics, no longer content to be just a passive observer and reporter.

And this was only the beginning for me.

Jeremiah stood back with Amelia and Grace, and my mom had taken Charlotte as I talked to the press, keeping them out of the public eye. That was something we agreed upon, and I made it clear to anyone who wanted to talk to me - my daughters were off-limits for photos.

I answered a few questions, then excused myself to spend the rest of the time with my family. Being in the public eye was exhausting, but I was better suited for it than Jeremiah.

"It's clear we've made the right choice in who ran for office," Jeremiah whispered into my ear.

I chuckled. "Damn straight we did."

Jeremiah was still working, but only when he wanted to. We had a nanny part-time, but mostly we raised our kids ourselves. Jeremiah worked from home a lot, and he seemed to like caring for the girls himself. I was home as much as I could be, making sure I never neglected my family for my career. Liberty was a town that understood family came first; it was never an issue. I was almost always home for dinner, and I would always put the girls to bed with Jeremiah. Some things were non-negotiable.

Jeremiah enjoyed building things again. He worked with Kellen and Grant, and they had a woodworking business making cabinets and furniture and whatnot. It made him happy. Happier than working as the mayor.

Jeremiah captured my attention by brushing against me since his hands were full of almost toddlers. "Come here, I want to show you something."

We slipped away from the prying eyes of the press and the people, behind some trees and near the small stream that ran down from the mountains. Somehow, Jeremiah had found a private little alcove, a piece of Heaven.

"This is beautiful," I said, walking over to the stream. "Look at this, Char."

I turned the baby so she could see the stream, her little eyes taking it all in.

"That's not what I wanted to show you," Jeremiah said from behind me.

"Then what—" I turned around.

Amelia and Grace each held piece of paper in their tiny little hands. The two combined spelled out, "Will you marry our daddy?"

My heart nearly exploded in my chest. Jeremiah and I had talked about marriage someday. Life had just been so crazy that it kept getting put off.

He held up a box .

"Are you— Really?" I felt like a teenage girl. My knees went weak and I felt like this had to be a dream.

"Of course, Elle," he said. "You're the most beautiful woman, inside and out. You accomplish everything you set your mind to, and I'm so proud of you. We have a beautiful family, and even though we technically live like husband and wife, I thought it was high time we made it official. So what do you say? Will you marry me?"

Tears filled my eyes, and I rushed over to him. I stopped as he opened the ring box. My mother's engagement ring. He'd gotten permission from my mother, and she'd given him the ring my father had given to her. The ring that had been on her hand for as long as I can remember.

If I hadn't been crying before, I was now. Full on sobs, but they were tears of happiness. Complete and utter joy.

Jeremiah slipped the ring on my shaky finger. "So is that a yes?"

All this excitement, and I had forgotten to answer him. "Of course," I said, sniffling as I saw the diamond glistening on my hand. "I mean, yes. Of course I'll marry you."

We hugged as best we could with three babies, and Amelia and Grace even got into the act. They might not understand the meaning behind it yet, but they could sense our excitement. Grace tried to eat the paper with the engagement on it, which I had to carefully pry it from her hands. But that was life with three kids under the age of two.

It was wild and crazy sometimes, but I wouldn't have it any other way.

The End

Made in United States
Orlando, FL
15 October 2023

37906397R00125